S0-CPS-484

STREAKS OF SQUATTER LIFE, AND FAR-WEST SCENES

"Raising his hat and kissing his hand, he turned down the slope."—*Page* 41.

STREAKS
OF
SQUATTER LIFE,
AND
FAR-WEST SCENES.

BY

JOHN S. ROBB

A FACSIMILE REPRODUCTION

EDITED WITH AN INTRODUCTION AND NOTES

BY

JOHN FRANCIS McDERMOTT
Washington University

GAINESVILLE, FLORIDA
SCHOLARS' FACSIMILES & REPRINTS
1962

SCHOLARS' FACSIMILES & REPRINTS
118 N.W. 26TH STREET
GAINESVILLE, FLORIDA, U.S.A.
HARRY R. WARFEL, GENERAL EDITOR

REPRODUCED FROM A COPY OWNED BY

JOHN FRANCIS McDERMOTT

L. C. CATALOG CARD NUMBER: 62-7018

MANUFACTURED IN THE U.S.A.

LETTERPRESS BY J. N. ANZEL, INC.
PHOTOLITHOGRAPHY BY EDWARDS BROTHERS
BINDING BY UNIVERSAL-DIXIE BINDERY

INTRODUCTION

John S. Robb's *Streaks of Squatter Life,* like many others of its genre, is today a rare book because it was published as popular literature and sold for fifty cents. Cheaply printed, not many copies have survived the wear of more than a century. But its hard humor and its realistic glimpses of life in the early West are as entertaining and as illuminating now as when he wrote. Robb's touch was authentic, his contribution original. His place in literature is small but it is permanent. A new issue of his book is certainly his due.

I

The founding of William T. Porter's New York *Spirit of the Times* in 1831, the publication of A.B. Longstreet's *Georgia Scenes* in 1835, and the establishment of the New Orleans *Picayune* in 1836 were all events of first importance in the history of the humorous-realistic literature of the South and the West in the generation before Mark Twain. Equally important — though less recognized — was the founding of the St. Louis *Reveille* in July, 1844, for in the half-dozen years of its existence hundreds of tall tales and sketches of life and manners in the West were published in its columns, reprinted in its weekly edition, reprinted in the *Spirit of the Times,* reprinted again in Porter's anthologies (*The Big Bear of Arkansas,* 1845, and *A Quarter Race in Kentucky,* 1846), and reprinted once more by their authors as books. Sol Smith's *Theatrical Apprenticeship* (1845), John S. Robb's *Streaks of Squatter Life* (1847), and Joe Field's *The Drama in Pokerville* (1847) – co-equals of *Odd Leaves of a Swamp Doctor* (1843), *Major Jones' Courtship* (1843), *The Adventures of Simon Suggs* (1845), *The Mysteries of the Backwoods* (1846), and Porter's two collections in Carey and Hart's Library of Humorous American Works – all originated in the *Reveille.* Like Porter in New York, Charles Keemle, with two decades of St. Louis newspaper experience behind him, and Joseph M. Field, trained on the *Picayune,* encouraged many a man to "spread himself" in the vein "peculiar" to their pages. The enduring result was the *Weekly Reveille* with a literary content second in its time only to that of the *Spirit of the Times.*

John S. Robb, one of the most prolific of the *Reveille's* contributors, began life as a printer. The place and date of his birth remain unknown. It seems likely that he was born in Philadelphia and certain that he was trained as a "typo" or "jour" printer – and as such wandered over the country. From scattered references we learn that he was in Detroit in 1839 and that later he may have worked on the *Picayune* in New Orleans. In December, 1842, he was in St. Louis, editing the *Ledger,* a paper of which no issue is extant. After this publication collapsed, he worked for the St. Louis *Missouri Republican* as a printer, and in 1845 he was foreman of the *Reveille* composition department. Though he was a steady and welcomed contributor to the latter paper, it was not until the departure for Oregon of George L. Curry, an assistant editor of the *Reveille,* in April, 1846, that a place opened for Robb; he moved from composing room to editorial office. He continued on the *Reveille* staff until January, 1849, when, as special correspondent for his paper, he left for the gold fields with a small party of St. Louisans. He did not, however, return to St. Louis as expected but presently set up in Stockton, California, as publisher and editor of a newspaper. He died in San Francisco in 1856.

On the *Reveille* Robb's special talent for the feature story was evidently recognized, for he was frequently employed as a roving correspondent. When a new town was opened in southern Missouri opposite the mouth of the Ohio, Robb went down to cover the launching of the enterprise. When the making of moving panoramas of the Mississippi became the rage in 1848 (three were painted by St. Louis artists that year), Robb went north by excursion steamboat to Fort Snelling, spent ten days visiting Captain and Mrs. Seth Eastman at that post and looking at "Indian land," and then accompanied Henry Lewis in his sketching boat down the river — reporting all these scenes and actions in the *Reveille.* A railroad convention in Chicago, a political meeting in Louisville, a steamboat trip down the Mississippi, a journey to Philadelphia and New York – all brought a flow of news-letters. In intervals he would report "St. Louis in Patches" and write "Views of Home," feature stories which in themselves make a record of considerable interest today.

All this, however sprightly and observant, was regular journalism. As a literary writer Robb had made his reputation a year and a half before he was brought out of the composing room. The sketches that went into *Streaks of Squatter Life* were "the production of the few short hours outside of *eight* in the morning and *ten* at night, the time between being occupied by arduous duties which almost forbid thought, save of themselves." His first contribution to the *Reveille* over the signature "Solitaire," " 'Not a Drop More, Major, Unless It's Sweeten'd' " (October 21, 1844), forecast the line of rough, backcountry humor that he would chiefly follow.

His second prose piece, the recounting of a practical joke in which a man in a St. Louis bar convinced a Sucker from Illinois, to his horror, that he had swallowed a living oyster, appeared in the *Weekly Reveille* of December 9, 1844. It was promptly reprinted in *The Spirit of the Times* (January 18, 1845) and in April following found book publication in *The Big Bear of Arkansas.* Porter assumed the pseudonymous author to be Joe Field but in *The Spirit* for April 19 corrected his error. This little skit established Robb as a writer. Henceforth he was "Solitaire, the Author of 'Swallowing Oysters Alive'," a tag which was to be used by his publishers on the title page of his book.

By the close of 1845 Robb had contributed at least eighteen more such pieces to the *Reveille.* That he was read and appreciated "at the East" now became clear. "We are glad to learn," said the St. Louis *American* on January 12, 1846, "that Mr. Robb, who has written many sprightly articles under the above signature [Solitaire], has *'had a call'* from Messrs. Carey & Hart, of Philadelphia, to prepare a book of sketches for their press. We consider it quite a compliment, for publishers of so much discernment, to solicit a work of this kind from a newspaper writer. It shows, however, that the articles possess unusual merit." The *Weekly Reveille* of the same date, pointing out that Robb had been introduced to the public through its columns, had "a feeling of peculiar pride in this matter [because Solitaire was] . . . a practical *typo,* foreman in the composition department of this journal." The *Missouri Republican,* too, joined in the praise of "an old familiar of our own."

In response to the "call" Robb gathered up seventeen sketches published in the *Reveille* between October 21, 1844, and January 5, 1846, two of which had been reprinted in the *Reveille* after earlier publication elsewhere. Some or all of the remaining seven pieces were written "expressly" for the volume, and four of these in turn were reprinted from *Streaks* in the *Reveille.*

Confusion about the date of publication of Robb's book has arisen because some copies of the most commonly available edition (1858) bear a copyright entry date of 1843 and others of 1846. That the work was first issued in April, 1847, is clear from statements in the *Reveille*. On March 22 it published "Old Sugar! The Standing Candidate," described as "a sketch from a new work shortly to be issued in Carey & Hart's 'Library of American Humorous Works, entitled 'Streaks of Squatter Life and Far West Scenes,' by John S. Robb, Esq. of the St. Louis *Reveille,* author of 'Swallowing Oysters Alive'." On May 10 the *Reveille* reprinted "Courting in French Hollow" from "Robb's volume of stories just published by Carey and Hart." The rare original edition carries the 1846 copyright (reproduced here from the copy in the Sinclair Hamilton Collection, Princeton University Library).

The eight wood engravings were drawn by F.O.C. Darley (1822-1888), the most prolific and vigorous book illustrator of nineteenth-century United States, who illustrated all the volumes in Carey and Hart's Library of Humorous American Works.

II

"The west," Robb declared in his preface, "abounds with incident and humor, and the observer must lack an eye for the comic who can look upon the panorama of western life without being tempted to laugh. It would indeed seem that the nearer sundown, the more original the character and odd the expression, as if the sun, with his departing beams, had shed a new feature upon the back-woods inhabitants. This oddity and originality has often attracted my attention and contributed to my amusement; . . . every step of the pioneer's progress has been marked with incidents, humorous and thrilling, which wait but the wizard spell of a bright mind and able pen to call them from misty traditions, and clothe them with speaking life." Robb was too modest to think his a "wizard spell" – he merely hoped that his "hasty efforts" would "aid to awaken attention and attract skillful pens to this original and striking field of literature."

Some of the sketches in *Streaks of Squatter Life and Far-West Scenes. A Series of Humorous Sketches Descriptive of Incidents and Characters in the Wild West. To Which Are Added Other Miscellaneous Pieces* are assuredly "miscellaneous" and have nothing to do with squatter life or the Far West. Two of these, intended for social satire, can be dismissed quickly: "Who Are They?" was concerned with the American passion for imposing social background; "Letters from a Baby" "exposed" neglect of infants by their mothers. Several other pieces "of a local character" probably did contribute to the amusement of St. Louis readers. "A Spiritual Sister" was a joke on Sol Smith; "Natural Acting" related an anecdote about Dan Marble, the comic actor, who was well known in St. Louis and to Robb; "Telegraphing an Express" was a little feature story about the way Colonel Keemle on one occasion scooped the president's message to Congress for the *Reveille;* and "George Munday" was a sketch about a wandering "prophet."

Of more general appeal were several old standbys in humor. "Settlement Fun," placed in Liberty, Missouri, on the frontier, had nothing really to do with the Far West, since it was built upon the admiration stirred in the women there by the little shoemaker who had begot triplets. "The Death Struggle" was likewise given frontier locale, but the amusement lies rather in the rivalry of two shoemakers who might live in any village than in realistic depiction. "Doing a Landlord" is the old tale of a rogue managing to scrounge first a dinner and then six months' credit at a hotel by the display of a borrowed $1,000 bill; it was laid in St. Louis presumably because it was printed in a St. Louis newspaper.

Something slightly more western is to be found in the opening and longest story, "The Western Wanderings of a Typo," the high points of which describe the farcical experiences of a young journeyman printer as publisher and editor, for a very short time, in Indiana and an equally ludicrous scene at an election in Illinois. Western in spirit, too, are several practical joke pieces. "A Canal Adventure" takes place on the Erie Canal, but the manner in which the Yankee, Irish, and Western types unite to overwhelm the dandy is in the spirit of Mark Twain's first skit, "The Dandy Frightening the Squatter." "An Emigrant's Perils" has some originality in its picture of a traveler, headed for the Missouri, being pulled about by two steamboat runners on the St. Louis levee. A joke more elaborately sustained, with the authentic turn of western narrative, is the story of the cure wrought in a hard-drinking steamboat engineer by the belief of his wife in William Miller's prophecy of the end of the world and by the practical jesting of the captain and the clerk.

The story of engineer Tom Bagnall's moment in hell in "The Second Advent" would itself have qualified Robb for first-class membership in the "western humorists' guild," but he was less interested in the river types than in the backwoods settler, whom he thought "a free and jovial character, inclined to mirth rather than evil, and when he encounters his fellow man at a barbacue, election, log-rolling, or frolic, he is more disposed to join in a feeling of hilarity on the occasion, than to participate in wrong or outrage." In the stories about the backcountry man Robb transcends the joke and the mere anecdote and makes a contribution to the literature of the frontier. These are no longer mere funny bits or brief feature stories but creative fictions.

Two are tall tales. "A Cat Story" recounts the manner in which a man, who has fallen from a steamboat into the Mississippi and is slowly sinking in the mud, saves himself by seizing hold of the tail of a Mississippi catfish six feet long. "Fun with a 'Bar'" calls to mind the more famous "Big Bar of Arkansas," but it is an original and brilliantly amusing sketch of frontier life. Dan Elkhorn, a Missouri hunter, entertains his companion mountain men on the Upper Platte with the tale of how his courting a girl led him to spend a night on a snag in the Missouri with a bear for a companion, and how, when he went hunting the bear the next day, he found him dead in the crotch of a tree: "that owdacious varmint, knowin' I'd kill him for his trick, jest climbed up thar whar I could easy find him, and died to spite me!"

Politics provided the materials for two of Robb's best pieces. "The Standing Candidate" pictures a drunk old hanger-on at a political barbacue in just such a scene as George Caleb Bingham painted in his *Stump Orator* at this same time (it was very likely Robb who wrote the "review" of this picture that appeared in the *Reveille* on December 6, 1847). As the first squatter in the county "Old Sugar" had been a "standing candidate" for the legislature at every election. It was his custom to appear at gatherings of the "sovereigns" with his portable "grocery," make the other candidates drink with him, and comment very freely on the speakers of the day, to the thorough entertainment of many of the listeners. "Hoss Allen's Apology" purports to tell one of the many "rich jokes" related about the political encounters of two candidates for the governorship of Missouri: "Edwards being slow, dignified and methodical, while Hoss tosses dignity to the winds, and comes right down to a free and easy familiarity with the 'boys'." In this story Hoss had the best of the joke – but he lost the election.

Four courtship stories are as hilariously effective as anything Robb's contemporaries wrote. In "Nettle Bottom Ball" the "boys" of the Bottom got up a ball; the high point is reached when Betsy Jones, dressing in the upper story of her father's cabin, falls through the thin flooring "without any thin' on yearth on her but one of these *starn cushins . . . flat into a pan of mush!"* In "Yaller Pledges" the rival manages to convince the girl that the pledges of love the narrator has promised to bring back from New Orleans are mulatto children out of his past. "Seth Tinder's First Courtship" and "Courting in French Hollow," both laid in St. Louis, recount similar discomfitures.

Only one story touches on the "dark streaks" of squatter life. "The Pre-emption Right" shows Dick Kelsey and his Negro slave, who is his friend as much as his servant, living ideally until Congress has passed the pre-emption law. The resulting inflow of emigrants brings a landgrabber who attempts to take Kelsey's claim. A story of violence develops in which the villain tries to kill Kelsey but is finally himself shot by the squatter. Allowing for certain sentimentality, it is a hard and realistic piece without a turn of humor.

Robb made the point in his preface that his stories had been "written as much for the reader's amusement as illustrations of odd incidents and character." Certainly as pictures of some phases of frontier life they are fully successful. Scene, incident, tone, and detail all ring true. The humor is decidely a masculine one, rude and rough, without delicacy or subtlety, but it amused readers of the *Reveille* and *The Spirit of the Times* and, at its best, stirs men to laugh today.

Though "Solitaire" contributed many more excellent sketches to the *Reveille,* and *The Spirit of the Times* continued to reprint them, he did not publish another book, but his one little volume of humorous and realistic vignettes has made a permanent place for him in the history of the literature produced on the frontier before the Civil War.

John Francis McDermott

Washington University
22 December 1960

STREAKS

OF

SQUATTER LIFE,

AND

FAR-WEST SCENES.

A SERIES OF HUMOROUS SKETCHES DESCRIPTIVE OF INCIDENTS AND CHARACTER IN THE WILD WEST.

TO WHICH ARE ADDED

OTHER MISCELLANEOUS PIECES.

BY "SOLITAIRE,"

(JOHN S. ROBB, OF ST. LOUIS, MO.,)

AUTHOR OF "SWALLOWING OYSTERS ALIVE."

Dan Elkhorn.—I've seen more *fun* in these yeur diggins than would fill a *book!*
Solitaire.—Can I persuade you, Dan, to relate those scenes to me?
Dan.—Well, *hoss*, I won't do anythin' else!

PHILADELPHIA:

CAREY AND HART.

1847.

ORIGINAL TITLE PAGE

Printed by T. K. & P. G. Collins

ORIGINAL COPYRIGHT PAGE

From WILLIAM T. PORTER, ed., *The Big Bear of Arkansas* (Philadelphia: Carey and Hart, 1845), pp. 80-86. Courtesy of St. Louis Mercantile Library.

SWALLOWING AN OYSTER ALIVE,

A STORY OF ILLINOIS—BY A MISSOURIAN.

We should hate to bet "*Straws*" that J. M. Field, the principal editor of the St. Louis "Revillé," was not the writer of the following story. Unlike his late brother "Poor Mat"—better known as "Phazma"—who recently died at sea, our friend "Joe" is full of fun and frolic, and ready to "go at any thing in the ring—from pitch-and-toss to manslaughter!" When he became an editor by profession, the stage sustained a material loss. He was indeed one of "the best actors in the world, either for tragedy, comedy, history, pastoral, pastoral-comical, historical-pastoral, tragical-historical, tragical-comical-historical-pastoral, scene undividable, or poem unlimited." For several years he has been a contributor to the periodical press; but quite recently he has embarked in the enterprise of a new daily journal at St. Louis, which appears to have succeeded almost beyond his hopes. The annexed sketch is "a taste of the quality" of the "Revillé" and himself.

AT a late hour, the other night, the door of an oyster house in our city was thrust open, and in stalked a hero from the Sucker state. He was quite six feet high, spare, somewhat stooped, with a hungry, anxious countenance, and his hands pushed clear down to the bottom of his breeches pockets. His outer covering was hard to define, but after surveying it minutely, we came to the conclusion that his suit had been made in his boyhood, of a dingy yellow linsey-wolsey, and that, having sprouted up with astonishing rapidity, he had been forced to piece it out with all colours, in order to keep pace with his body. In spite of his exertions, however, he had fallen in arrears about a foot of the necessary length, and, consequently, stuck that far through his inexpressibles. His crop of hair was surmounted by the funniest little seal-skin cap imaginable. After taking a position, he indulged in a long stare at the man opening the *bivalves*, and slowly ejaculated—"isters?"

"Yes, sir," responded the attentive operator,—"and fine ones they are, too."

"Well, I've heard of isters afore," says he, "but this is the fust time I've seed 'm, and *pre-haps* I'll know what *thar* made of afore I git out of town.

Having expressed this desperate intention, he cautiously approached the plate and scrutinized the uncased shell-fish with a gravity and interest which would have done honour to the most illustrious searcher into the hidden mysteries of nature. At length he began to soliloquize on the difficulty of getting them out, and how queer they looked when out.

"I never seed any thin' hold on so—takes an amazin' site of screwin, hoss, to get 'em out, and aint they slick and slip'ry when they does come? Smooth as an eel! I've a good mind to give that feller lodgin', jist to realize the effects, as uncle Jess used to say about speckalation."

"Well, sir," was the reply, "down with two bits, and you can have a dozen."

"Two bits!" exclaimed the Sucker, "now come, that's stickin' it on rite strong, hoss, for *isters*. A dozen on 'em aint nothin' to a chicken, and there's no gettin' more'n a picayune a piece for *them*. I've only realized forty-five picayunes on my first ventur' to St. Louis. I'll tell you what, I'll gin you two chickens for a dozen, if you'll conclude to deal."

A wag, who was standing by indulging in a dozen, winked to the attendant to shell out, and the offer was accepted.

"Now mind," repeated the Sucker, "all fair—two chickens for a dozen—you're a witness, mister," turning at the same time to the wag; "none of your tricks, for I've heard that your city fellers are mity slip'ry coons."

The bargain being fairly understood, our Sucker squared himself for the onset; deliberately put off his seal-skin, tucked up his sleeves, and, fork in hand, awaited the appearance of No. 1. It came—he saw—and quickly it was bolted! A moment's dreadful pause ensued. The wag dropped his knife and fork with a look of mingled amazement and horror—something akin to Shakspeare's Hamlet on seeing his daddy's ghost—while he burst into the exclamation—

"Swallowed alive, as I'm a Christian!"

Our Sucker hero had opened his mouth with pleasure a moment before, but now it *stood* open. Fear—a horrid dread of he didn't know what—a consciousness that all was'nt right, and ignorant of the extent of the wrong—the uncertainty of the moment was terrible. Urged to desperation, he faultered out—

"What on earth's the row?"

"Did you swallow it alive?" inquired the wag.

"O gracious!—what'ill I do?—It's got hold of my innards already, and I'm dead as a chicken!— do somethin' for me, do— don't let the infernal sea-toad eat me afore your eyes."

"I swallowed it jest as he gin it to me!" shouted the Sucker.

"You're a dead man!" exclaimed his anxious friend, "the creature is alive, and will eat right through you," added he, in a most hopeless tone.

"Get a pizen pump and pump it out!" screamed the Sucker, in a frenzy, his eyes fairly starting from their sockets. "O gracious!—what'ill I do?—It's got holds of my innards already, and I'm dead as a chicken!—do somethin' for me, do—don't let the infernal sea-toad eat me afore your eyes."

"Why don't you put some of this on it?" inquired the wag, pointing to a bottle of strong pepper-sauce.

The hint was enough—the Sucker, upon the instant, seized the bottle, and desperately wrenching out the cork, swallowed half the contents at a draught. He fairly squealed from its effects, and gasped and blowed, and pitched, and twisted, as if it were coursing through him with electric effect, while at the same time his eyes ran a stream of tears. At length becoming a little composed, his waggish adviser approached, almost bursting with suppressed laughter, and inquired,—

"How are you now old fellow—did you kill it?"

"Well, I did, hoss'—ugh, ugh o-o-o my inards. If that *ister* critter's dyin' agonies didn't stir a 'ruption in me equal to a small arthquake, then 'taint no use sayin' it—it squirmed like a sarpent, when that killin' stuff touched it; hu'—and here with a countenance made up of suppressed agony and present determination, he paused to give force to his words, and slowly and deliberately remarked, "If you git two chickens from me for that live animal, I'm d—d!" and seizing his seal-skin he vanished.

The shout of laughter, and the contortions of the company at this finale, would have made a spectator believe that they had all been *swallowing oysters alive.*

BIBLIOGRAPHY

EDITIONS

1. *Streaks of Squatter Life, and Far-West Scenes. A Series of Humorous Sketches Descriptive of Incidents and Character in the Wild West. To which are added Other Miscellaneous Pieces.* By "Solitaire," (John S. Robb, of St. Louis, Mo.,) author of "Swallowing Oysters Alive." Philadelphia: Carey and Hart. 1847. On cover: Carey & Hart's Library of Humorous American Works

Copies: Library of Congress, Princeton University Library.

2. *The Swamp Doctor's Adventures in the South-west. Containing the Whole of the Louisiana Swamp Doctor; Streaks of Squatter Life and Far-Western Scenes; in a Series of Forty-two Humorous Southern and Western Sketches, Descriptive of Incidents and Character.* By "Madison Tensas," M.D., and "Solitaire," (John S. Robb, of St. Louis, Mo.) Author of "Swallowing Oysters Alive," Etc. With Fourteen Illustrations, from Original Designs by Darley. Philadelphia, T. B. Peterson and Brothers, n. d. On reverse of title: Entered according Act of Congress, in the year 1858, by T. B. Peterson. . . On front cover: Peterson's Illustrated Uniform Edition of Humorous American Works

There are in addition separate title pages for *The Swamp Doctor* and for *Streaks* identical with those of the original issue except for a change in the name of the publisher and an omission of the date. The verso of both in my copy bears the copyright date of 1843, the printer repeating in error the correct date for *The Swamp Doctor*. In the copies in the Mercantile Library of St. Louis and the Missouri Historical Society, obviously later printings, the copyright date is 1846.

3. *Western Scenes; or, Life on the Prairie. A Series of Humorous Sketches Descriptive of Incidents and Character in the Wild West. To which are added other Miscellaneous Pieces.* By "Solitaire," (John S. Robb, of St. Louis, Mo.) Author of "Swallowing Oysters Alive." Philadelphia, T. B Peterson and Brothers, n.d. Copyright entry: 1858.

Copy: Mercantile Library of St. Louis (original covers missing).

Note: the text of all editions is identical: the same stereotype plates were used.

SERIAL PUBLICATION

Very few issues of the daily *Reveille* are extant. All references here are to the *Weekly Reveille* (the pages of which are continuously numbered). Files consulted are in the Missouri Historical Society and the Mercantile Library of St. Louis. Except as indicated, all titles were published over the signature "Solitaire."

"The Western Wanderings of a Typo." Not located.

" 'Not a Drop More, Major, Unless It's Sweeten'd.' " October 21, 1844, p. 113. Not signed.

"Nettle Bottom Ball." May 19, 1845, p. 353. In *Spirit*, June 7, 185 (XV, 169).

"A Cat Story." June 23, 1845, p. 397. In *Spirit*, July 5, 1845 (XV, 217).

"A Spiritual Sister." September 29, 1845, p. 600. In *Spirit*, October 18, 1845 (XV, 397).

"Hoss Allen's Apology." Reprinted from *Streaks* in *Reveille*, May 17, 1847, pp. 1278-79.

"Natural Acting." August 11, 1845, p. 449. In *Spirit*, August 23, 1845 (XV, 299).

"A Canal Adventure." February 3, 1845, p. 233. In *Spirit*, February 22, 1845 (XIV, 615).

"The Standing Candidate." Reprinted from *Streaks* in *Reveille*, March 22, 1847, p. 1211.

"An Emigrant's Perils." June 9, 1845, p. 377. In *Spirit*, July 19, 1845 (XV, 238).

"Fun with a 'Bar'." December 8, 1845, p. 675. In *Spirit*, December 20, 1845 (XV, 503).

"Telegraphing an Express." December 22, 1845, p. 691.

"The Pre-Emption Right." November 17, 1845, pp. 656-657. Reprinted in *Reveille* from *Neal's Philadelphia Saturday Gazette*. In *Spirit*, November 8, 1845 (XV, 437).

"Yaller Pledges." Reprinted from *Streaks* in *Reveille*, July 12, 1847, p. 1341.

"George Munday." March 3, 1845, p. 265. Not signed. In *Spirit*, March 15, 1845 (XV, 21).

"Courting in French Hollow." Reprinted from *Streaks* in *Reveille*, May 10, 1847, p. 1267.

"The Second Advent." Not located.

"Settlement Fun." Not located. A series of eight letters under this title was run in the *Reveille* in April-July, 1846, but the letter in *Streaks* was not one of this group.

" 'Doing' a Landlord." September 15, 1845, p. 489. In *Spirit*, October 4, 1845 (XV, 372).

"Who Is Sir George Simpson?" May 12, 1845, p. 349; there entitled "The 'Consul at Panama's' Friend, Sir George Simpson." Not signed.

"Letters from a Baby." July 21, 1845, p. 425; p. 429; August 4, p. 443; October 13, p. 616; January 5, 1846, p. 707. The third letter in this series, headed "The Last" in the *Reveille,* was omitted from *Streaks;* several others were slightly edited.

"Seth Tinder's First Courtship." December 30, 1844, p. 193.

"The Death Struggle." June 23, 1845, p. 393. In *Spirit,* July 26, 1845 (XV, 257).

" 'Who Are They?' " June 9, 1845, p. 379. Reprinted in *Reveille* from the *Chaplet of Mercy.* In *Spirit,* June 14, 1845 (XV, 181).

SOURCES TO CONSULT

Barrett, Mary Helen. *A Study of John S. Robb, a Southwest Humorist.* M. A. Thesis, University of Missouri, 1950, mimeograph edition.

Blair, Walter. *Native American Humor (1800-1900).* New York: American Book Company, 1937.

Meine, Franklin J. *Tall Tales of the Southwest.* New York: Alfred A. Knopf, 1930.

McDermott, John Francis. "Gold Fever: The Letters of 'Solitaire,' Goldrush Correspondent of '49," *Missouri Historical Society Bulletin,* V, 115-126, 211-223, 316-331, VI, 34-43 (January-October, 1949).

———. "A Journalist at Old Fort Snelling: Some Letters of "Solitaire' Robb," *Minnesota History,* XXXI, 209-221 (December, 1950).

——— *The Lost Panoramas of the Mississippi.* Chicago: The University of Chicago Press, 1958.

Spotts, Carle Brooks. "The Development of Fiction on the Missouri Frontier," *Missouri Historical Review,* 104-108 (January, 1935).

Yates, Norris W. *William T. Porter and "The Spirit of the Times."* Baton Rouge: Louisiana State University Press, 1957.

NOTES

P. 15. Joseph Gales and William W. Seaton were the publishers of the Washington, D. C., *National Intelligencer;* Frank P. Blair and John C. Rives, of the Washington *Globe.*

Pp. 31-32. Thomas Ritchie, Richmond *Enquirer;* John H. Pleasants, Washington *Whig;* Frank P. Blair, Washington *Globe;* Joseph Gales, Washington *National Intelligencer;* Joseph Ripley Chandler, Philadelphia *North American;* George D. Prentice, Louisville *Journal;* Joseph Clay Neal, Philadelphia *Saturday Gazette.*

P. 67. That Sol Smith – lawyer, writer, actor-manager of St. Louis – was frequently mistaken for a preacher was a standing joke, even with Sol himself. See his "My First and Last Sermon" in *Theatrical Management in the West and South for Thirty Years* (New York: Harper and Brothers, 1868), 65-69.

P. 70. Hoss Allen was Circuit Judge Charles H. Allen, who came from Kentucky about 1830 to Palmyra, Missouri, and died there in 1862. The town of Benton was and is the county seat of Benton County. Though Allen had the best of the story, John C. Edwards (1806-1888) was elected governor of Missouri (1844).

P. 83. Danforth Marble (1810-1849), then a famous Yankee comic.

P. 91. "Buffalo Head, Nianga County, Missouri." Buffalo is the county seat of Dallas County through which the Niangua River flows north.

P. 113. Col. K. was Colonel Charles Keemle, senior editor of the *Reveille,* to whom Robb dedicated his book.

P. 139. On March 15, 1845, *The Spirit of the Times* reprinted this sketch, omitting the first four paragraphs, and crediting it incorrectly to Joe Field. The introductory note read "This eccentric genius, who is now in Louisville, Ky., is expected in St. Louis, shortly; accordingly, Field, of the Reveille, prepares his fellow citizens to anticipate rare fun by recounting one of the Prophet's freaks."

P. 148. William Miller, founder of the Millerites, who predicted the destruction of the world in April, 1843.

P. 166. Sir George Simpson, of the Hudson's Bay Company, famous as a traveler.

P. 172. The Lambert Family were "Mammoth Boys," according to Barnum's advertisements.

P. 172. The Missourium was a super-mastodon fifteen feet high created by Albert Koch, proprietor of the St. Louis Museum, in 1840 from bones he dug up in Jefferson County, Missouri; eventually he sold one Missourium to the British Museum and another to the royal museum in Berlin. For him and it see my "Dr. Koch's Wonderful Fossils," *Missouri Histroical Society Bulletin,* IV, 233-256 (July, 1948).

P. 175. Robb is obviously making free with the names of friends. For Charley Wilgus, read Asa; for Asa Keemle, read Charles; for Augustus Vinton, read O. M.; for Edward Shade, read John; for John Charless, read Edward; for Christopher Wigery, read John Widgery; for John Dalrymple, read W. W.; for Wallace Finney, read either John or William; for Colton A. Presbury Jr., read G. G.; for Presbury G. A. Colton, read George A. Colton; for Rucker Smith, read Alfred M. Rucker Smith; for O. M. Ridgely, read F. R.

STREAKS

OF

SQUATTER LIFE,

AND

FAR-WEST SCENES.

A SERIES OF HUMOROUS SKETCHES DESCRIPTIVE OF INCIDENTS AND CHARACTER IN THE WILD WEST.

TO WHICH ARE ADDED

OTHER MISCELLANEOUS PIECES.

BY "SOLITAIRE,"

(JOHN S. ROBB, OF ST. LOUIS, MO.,)

AUTHOR OF "SWALLOWING OYSTERS ALIVE."

Dan Elkhorn.—I've seen more *fun* in these yeur diggins than would fill a ***book***
Solitaire.—Can I persuade you, Dan, to relate those scenes to me?
Dan.—Well, *hoss*, I won't do anythin' else!

Philadelphia:
T. B. PETERSON AND BROTHERS
306 CHESTNUT STREET.

COLLINS, PRINTER.

DEDICATION.

To Col. Charles Keemle.

Permit me, my friend, to dedicate to you these pages, the first production of my pen in the field of western literature, and allow me to say, that your own graphic relations of far-west scenes, witnessed when this now giant territory was in its infancy, has contributed much to illustrate for me the striking features of western character. You may be set down as one, who has not only been a dweller in the wilds since its primitive days, but an observer of its progress in every stage, from the semi-civilised state until the refinement of polished life has usurped the wilderness. Through this period of transition *you* have stood unchanged, and that generous and noble nature, which induced the Indian chieftain, in by-gone days, to style you as the "Gray Eagle" of the forest, calls forth this humble tribute of regard from your friend.

John S. Robb.

"Sich another man as that major," says she, "aint nowhere! and sich a mixtur' as *he does* make is temptin' to temp'rance lect'rers!"—*Page* 57.

CONTENTS.

PREFACE.

In offering the following sketches to the public, I feel somewhat like the hoosier candidate described his sensations, when he first essayed to deliver a *stump speech:* "I felt," said he, "that ef I could ony git the beginnin' out—ef I could ony say '*fellar citizens!*' that arter that it 'ud go jest as easy as corn shuckin'!" So with your humble servant, if this my first effort at book making should meet with favor, I feel that a second attempt would be a pleasing task. To all adventurers in the field of literature the slightest encouragement is a shower of success—in my own case a *smile* upon my effort will swell in my estimation to a downright "*snigger*." The commendation which was bestowed upon the sketch of "Swallowing Oysters Alive," was some evidence that it tickled the public taste, and, of course, its wide approval tickled the fancy of the author; so if this collection be an *infliction* upon the reading public's taste, they have themselves to blame—they offered the temptation.

It is unnecessary for me to apologise for their *style*, for to pretend a capability to furnish any better, I *don't* —and their finish will be excused when I state, they are the productions of the few short hours outside of *eight* in the morning and *ten* at night, the time between being occupied by arduous duties which almost forbid thought, save of themselves.

The west abounds with incident and humor, and the observer must lack an eye for the comic who can look upon the panorama of western life without being tempted to laugh. It would indeed seem that the nearer sundown, the more original the character and odd the expression, as if the sun, with his departing beams, had shed a new feature upon the back-woods inhabitants. This oddity and originality has often attracted my attention and contributed to my amusement, and I have wondered why the finished and graphic writers of our country so seldom sought material from this inviting field. The idea of ever attempting to develope any portion of this mine of incident and character, with my feeble pen, has but recently been flattered into existence, and if my hasty efforts but aid to awaken attention and attract skilful pens to this original and striking field of literature, my highest ambition is attained. The amusing delineations of THORPE, HOOPER, FIELD, SOL SMITH, and others, who have with abler pens developed these incidents of western life, and the avidity with which their sketches have been read, give assurance that the rivers and valleys of this western land will no longer be neglected. That it here abounds as plentiful as the minerals within its bosom, there is no question, for every step of the pioneer's progress has been marked with incidents, humorous and thrilling, which wait but the wizard spell of a bright mind and able pen to call them from misty tradition, and clothe them with speaking life.

It is true there are dark streaks in western life, as well as light ones, as where in human society exists the one without the other; but, in their relation, the future historian of the wilds should be careful to distinguish between the actual settler and the *border harpy*. The acts of this latter class have often thrilled the refined mind with horror, and brought condemnation upon the pioneer, while a wide distinction exists between the two characters. The *harpy* is generally some worthless and criminal character, who, having to flee from more populous districts, seeks refuge at the outskirts of civilization, and there preys alike upon the red man and unsuspecting settler. There have been instances where, after a long career of depredation, these offenders have aroused the vengeance of the back-woods settler, when his punishment became as sweeping as his hospitality had before been warm and unsuspecting. In general, however, the western *squatter* is a free and jovial character, inclined to mirth rather than evil, and when he encounters his fellow man at a barbecue, election, log-rolling, or frolic, he is more disposed to join in a feeling of hilarity on the occasion, than to participate in wrong or outrage. An encounter with the hostile red skins, or the wild animals of the forest is to him pleasurable excitement, and his fireside or camp-fire is rich with story of perilous adventure, and which seems only worthy of his remembrance, when fearfully hazardous in incident.

Appended to these Western Sketches will be found several of a satirical and humorous character, which have met with some favor; though of a local character, they may contribute to the amusement of the reader, and if so, the object for which they were written has been attained.

In conclusion, allow me to add, that the within pages are written as much for the reader's amusement as the illustration of odd incidents and character, and if they fail in this, they fail altogether;—it is certain I have *tried* to be *funny*, and not to succeed in such an effort is the most hopeless of all literary failures. I shall leave the decision of this, to me momentous, question, to the indulgence of the public, and hold myself ready to "back out" if they decree it, or attempt a better effort under their approving smile.

A word to the *critics*:—Gentlemen, I have a high respect for you, and some little fear, and I, therefore, beg of you to touch me lightly—if you touch me at all; or, in the language of the Irish pupil, when about to receive a thrashing from his tutor;—"If you can't be *aisy*, be as aisy as you *can!*"

THE AUTHOR.

STREAKS OF SQUATTER LIFE,

AND

FAR-WEST SCENES.

THE WESTERN WANDERINGS OF A TYPO.

CHAPTER I.

THE WAY HE WAS "BROUGHT UP."

JOHN EARL, the subject of our story, was a true and veritable specimen of the genus *Jour Printer*,—intelligent, reckless, witty, improvident, competent, and unsteady,—floating on the great sea of life, regardless of either its winds or tides,—but little troubled about the present, and perfectly indifferent as to the future. John was the son of a Philadelphia printer, who died soon after his marriage, and the grief and destitution of our hero's mother so preyed upon her slender frame, that in giving birth to him she sunk under her sufferings—the wail of her offspring in this world was the knell which signalled her departure to another. That "the poor aids the poor," was a saying verified in John's case, for a poor shoemaker in the house adjoining his home took charge of the bereaved infant, and sheltered it beneath his humble roof. The worthy son of Crispin had none of his own to trouble him, and his wife and himself, as their little charge budded into prattling childhood, grew daily more fond of him, until our hero held at least his third of interest in the household. At his own request he was permitted to learn the same business his father had been bred to, and with many injunctions, and a good suit of clothes, he was consigned at a proper age to a master printer. Soon after his transfer to his new home, his adopted parents bade him farewell. The old shoemaker had become infected with the western fever for emigration, and after long and repeated consultations with his wife, had concluded to depart to the land of rapid fortunes and unbounded enterprise. The parting was affectionate, and after many fond wishes for each other's happiness, our hero was left to the mercies of the "Art preservative." We need not say that he grew wise in its mysteries, we will assume it as a matter of course. John was, or rather grew to be of a happy disposition, and viewed life as something resembling Pat's *pig*, a compound of alternate streaks of *fat* and *lean*, and whenever fortune looked through her blue spectacles upon his progress, he always set it down as his streak of lean, and grew happy amid his distresses, under the firm belief that his alternate slice of fat was next in order. He was a philosopher in the true sense of the word, for he let no occurrence of life rumple the couch of his repose—if he didn't like his quarters he took up his store of earthly wealth upon the end of a stick, and travelled. At the period of which we write, John had tasted four or five years of the responsibility of manhood, and had, from the day of his freedom, been an occasional visiter to all the Atlantic cities; he had now grown tired of his old tramping ground, and turned his eye westward. Who knows, thought John, but I may find a Mount Arrarat in the new land whereon to rest *my* ark! "The west, aye," thought John, "that mighty corn field—that region of pork and plenty—land of the migrating sucker—haven of hope, and country of adventure, I stretch out my arms towards thee, take me up like a mother, and be kind to your new child."

Gathering up his shirt No. 2, and overcoat No. 1, into a handkerchief valise, and wending his way to a Baltimore steamer, he proceeded on board, deposited his bundle, and shook the dust of the city from his feet. From the deck of the steamer he looked out upon the mart of trade, covered with its busy hundreds, who were rushing to and fro, and running in and out of the great store-houses, like swarms of bees around their hives.

"Poor fellows," soliloquized John, "how soon old time will knock them over, and distribute all the honey they are toiling for among a new generation."

A ringing of the steamer's bell disturbed his musings, and all became, for a few minutes, bustle and confusion—the engine moved, and the paddles answered its clank with a splash, a moment more and they were moving in the stream, and wending their way past the rows of shipping. As the smoke of the city faded from their view, John turned about to look upon his fellow passengers; some looked pleased, as if the trip was one of pleasure; others sad, as if departing from joys; whilst a portion, discontented with what they had left, appeared determined to dislike what they were journeying to, and muttered their displeasure audibly. Standing alone, leaning over the rail, was a fine looking elderly gentleman, whose countenance wore an air of quiet content and goodness—it was, indeed, one of those inviting countenances that we sometimes see possessed by honorable old age, which tells of wise thought and kindly sympathy, instead of a callous heart and suspicious mind, and our hero selected its owner for a travelling acquaintance. Approaching him, and leaning over a rail by his side, he remarked,

"We are moving through the water, sir, with lightning speed."

This assertion being most palpable and manifest, the old gent remarked in turn that they *were* moving with rapidity. Having fully agreed upon this point, John ventured further to enquire, "If it had ever occurred to his mind that steamboats were a great invention, any how?" The old gentleman acknowledged "he had been forcibly struck with the fact." Now, these passes of conversation may appear to the reader as very trivial and commonplace, but let us assure him they led to important results—they broke the ice which lay between two bodies, and let their souls float into contact. John having, as it were, got hold of the cover of non-intercourse, which most travellers wear, just unfolded it at each corner, and by his wit, intelligence, and reckless gaiety, folded himself up next the old man's heart, and tucked the corners of the robe under him. The old man soon became delighted with our hero, and they became inseparable *compagnons du voyage*.

A small bell was rung, and immediately the clerk commenced taking up tickets. Here was an eventful period for John—he had not troubled himself with the necessary receipt for passage, for one very good reason—he had none of the needful to purchase it with; like all philosophers he had great faith in luck, and now resigned himself to her care.

"I'll take your ticket, sir," said the clerk.

"I wish you would," said John, "if you see it any where about me."

The clerk took a stare at our hero, and then remarked, "I have no time to jest, sir."

"Nor I any inclination;" added John, "the fact is, my friend, I've got no ticket, and as uncle Sam is my only existing relation, and as you have a contract with him, suppose you book me as one of his *males*."

"I say I have no time for jesting, sir," reiterated the clerk, in an angry tone, "so please to hand me your ticket."

"Well, then," continued John, "I'll have to let you into my secret, I see,—I'm an attaché of the press, on my road to Washington;—now, I suppose, its all right. You are aware if I am delayed, Gales and Seaton will be very angry, and Blair and Rives get in a pucker."

The clerk was here getting into a wrathy state, when John's old friend reached the clerk the amount of his passage, and he passed on. John objected, but the old man insisted upon lending it to him, and the matter of fare being settled they sped onward smoothly as before. "Here's a streak of *fat*," thought John, "for I have accidentally fell in with a travelling angel," and as some return for his generosity, he set about making himself particularly agreeable to his old companion. In the course of their conversation the old gent learned John's history, and that he was now on his way to Washington in search of business, to raise money enough to carry him west. His companion informed John that he was a western man, and invited him to bear him company to his home in Cleveland, Ohio; but our hero preferred the Mississippi country. He agreed, however, if he should fail in gaining business in Washington, to accompany him to Wheeling, provided he would increase the debt already incurred, and trust to the goddess, luck, for payment. After being assured that his company was considered worth double the sum, the matter was set at rest, and they entered Washington together.

The old man had business in the city, and proposed to our hero, that while he was transacting it, he should take a stroll through the offices and see what chance there was for employment, and afterwards meet him at the Capitol. They separated, and when they again met, according to appointment, our typo "reported no progress," so it was instantly agreed they should depart for Wheeling. As they gazed from the "spectator's gallery," John whispered to his companion:

"I know the mass of those patriots below, and rightly appreciate them, for I have been behind the curtain—have helped some of them to make good English of their speeches to Bunkum,—have seen their tricks to get office, and their tricks to keep them,—have seen the *way* the cat jumps, and seen it *jump* too; in short, I'm up to the whole 'wool pulling' system, and I advise them to go it while they can, for the people may one day find them out, and then their spreading here will end in a sprawl at home."

He had gradually grown warm in his soliloquy, until his voice became audible, when the speaker struck his hammer, the sergeant-at-arms started for the gallery, and John and his old friend started for the stairs.

On the next morning the two departed west, leaving

the seat of government and its official inhabitants, for the broad land of promise which lay beyond.

"What think you of the capital?" enquired the old gentleman, as they journeyed onward.

"The worst," answered our hero, and assuming a Timon of Athens attitude, he added, "I have turned my back upon it in disgust. It is a theatre of the worst passions in our nature—chicanery lurks within the cabinet, distrust and envy without, while fawning sycophancy environs it around and about. To sum it up, it is a little of government—a great deal of 'bunkum,' sprinkled with a high seasoning of political juggling, the whole of which has but one end and aim—the spoils of Uncle Sam."

"Bravo!" exclaimed his old friend, "you will have to get elected from some of the Western states, and set about cleaning the Augean stable."

"Not I," answered John. "It's too dirty a job, and besides, the sovereign people claim it as their peculiar privilege, let them smell it out for themselves."

Discussing thus, things political, they jogged on to their place of parting, without incident worthy of noting by the way. John still held to his desire of visiting the Mississippi country, and his old friend insisted on paying his expenses to Cincinnati, our hero easily yielded to his proposition, with the understanding that it was to be paid when they again met.

"I may one day see you in Cleveland," said John, "with fortune buckled on my back, and if it should be there, 'whether I will or no,' be assured I shall not cut my old friends."

The old man laughed at the careless abandon of

3

his young friend, insisted upon his calling upon him in Cleveland when he had become tired of strolling, and they parted with warm expressions of regard. Our hero having found a boat which drew so little water, that it would, as the captain said, "run up a tree with a drop of the element upon it," he embarked on board, and stretching his form out in one of the state-room berths, gave liberty to his thoughts, and wandered back in memory to his childhood. Vainly did his memory search for some kindred face to dwell upon; the only semblance to such was the old shoemaker and his wife; and next to them he placed his late companion,—for he and his adopted parents were the only beings in his recollection who had ever bestowed upon him disinterested, kindly regard. He felt that he had floated like a moat in the sunbeam, whithersoever the breeze listed, having no home where he might nestle in health, or lie down in when seized by affliction—no port opened its arms to his bark, nor had it any destination—because it had no *papers!* but floated upon the broad wave of life the sport of fortune—and a hard fortune at that. As these thoughts stole over his heart, it became sad, and for the first time in years its fountains filled up to overflowing, and poured its burning waters over his cheeks. The future was a matter of such uncertainty, that he did not care to think upon it, nor at that moment did he care what it might bring forth—if good, well; if evil, it would be but a change from one feature of hard fortune to another. In due course of time the queen city of the west appeared in the distance, and his heart revived as he gazed upon her young greatness—hope awoke from her short slumber to urge him forward to greater efforts. On landing he sought out a printing establishment, and at his first application fortune favored him—a streak of *fat* was waiting for his arrival in the pork city, so throwing off his coat, he was soon clicking the type to the tune of "better days" and here we shall leave him until our next chapter.

CHAPTER II.

AN ADVENTURE AMONG THE OFFICIALS.

Our hero passed about two months in the queen city, when the desire to move again attacked him, and with the impulse he shaped his way for the Hoosier state, alone, and on foot. He was in that peculiar state of mind, and pocket, which calls forth all the coolness and wisdom of the philosopher, and to strengthen him on his journey he called up to mind all those illustrious examples of his craft, who had entered strange towns barefooted, and after rose to eminence and distinctions; several of whom now figured conspicuously upon the stage of public action. Trudging along thus, now stopping by the roadside to rest and muse, again plodding onward; now weary and desponding, again cheered by the carolling of the wood songsters, he would flourish his staff with sovereign contempt for care, whistle—"While you are young, you should be gay," and fixing his hat tighter upon his brow step out again with a republican stride. Earth had on her gayest livery, and the rich foliage of the western forests fluttered in a gentle breeze; which also fanned the brow of the solitary wanderer, as he toiled up a rising hill in his pathway. On reaching the brow of this small eminence he looked down upon a flourishing town which lay in the valley below him, and his spirits rose as he gazed upon the national flag, invitingly fluttering from the top of a snug-looking hotel.

"Huzza for the old striped bunting!" shouted John, "there is luck wherever it waves supreme, and if I don't come across a streak of *fat* soon, to recompense me for the long *lean* one I have been enjoying, then 'republics are ungrateful,' and I shall join the aristocracy and declaim against them."

The village upon which John was gazing was at that particular period the scene of unusual commotion, anxious expectation, and great excitement—every inhabitant appeared on tiptoe about something. The porch of the hotel was occupied by a group of leading citizens of the town, among whom was the postmaster, the squire, the parson, a distinguished physician, a member of the bar, and sundry smaller dignitaries attached to the official stations of the county-seat. The blacksmith would every now and then quit his forge, step out of his shop, and wiping the sweat from his brow take a long and searching look up the road, and then returning, pound away at the heated iron with powerful energy. The popular shoemaker was leaning out of his window looking earnestly in the same direction as his neighbor—the girls were peeping through their windows in a state of expectancy, and the young bucks of the town, dressed in their best, were flitting about in sight of the fair inhabitants, or clustering in groups directly opposite the abode of certain village beauties, while the more juvenile portion of the community were throwing up dust in the street, and huzzaing in a most animated and enthusiastic manner—in short, the town was upon the eve of a great occasion. The member of congress, from that district, was expected to partake of a public dinner, on that day, at the principal hotel of the town of M., in the state of Indiana, and his constituents had prepared to give him a hearty reception on his return home, for the able manner in which he had defended their interests. He was expected every moment, and of course, the place was big with anticipation.

John wended his way unnoticed down the street, but observing everything—his keen eye discovered not only matter of interest in the commotion, but high promise—there was evidently something "out," for the throbbing town, the fluttering banner, and the anxious groups betrayed it. Entering the hotel where the principal citizens were assembled, John mingled with the throng in the bar room, and listened to learn the cause of the gathering; how did his heart swell within him (for it had plenty of room) when he heard that a public *dinner* was on the tapis, a real bona fide dinner, of fish, flesh, and fowl, with an abundance of good liquor. John determined to search out the location of that town upon the map, and mark it down in his remembrance as possessing a highly civilized community. The landlord's son, an urchin of about six years of age, was every now and then running into the hall, and then out into the street, huzzaing at every termination of his race, running against every body, and putting on all sorts of wild antics—he appeared to have "cut" his comrades in the street, and was going the enthusiastic on his own hook, as if fully impressed with the honors descending upon his father's house—him our hero fixed upon to learn particulars, and seizing him as he entered the hall, enquired who was coming to eat the dinner that day.

"Hey, why, don't you know?—I guess you're a fellar of the other party;—it's the Governor that's a comin'," and off dashed the young publican.

An alarm now drew the crowd in the bar room out to the porch, barkeeper and all, and a citizen having left his glass untasted upon the counter, while he went to see the matter of interest outside, John just took the liberty of tasting the contents, by way of a priming to nerve him for future contingencies, and, after, quietly strolled to the rear of the house, where discovering a darkey blacking boots, he stuck up his dust-covered extremities, and authoritatively ordered him to brush them up; the darkey obeyed, and a wash after, at the pump, brought out John's genius bright as a "new dollar"—to use his own expression, he was *"a full case and printed copy!"* While he was arranging his cravat in the sitting room, a shout rent the air which made the glass before him rattle. Again! again! huzza! and dashing down to the hotel came a barouche containing the guest, with the judge of the district, a member of legislature, and the county clerk. Huzza! shouted the village—huzza! shouted our hero,—*bang!* went a small swivel at the upper end of the town—white waved the ladies' handkerchiefs, and high swelled the heart of a nation's statesman. At that exciting moment the Indiana representative loomed upon the public eye almost majestic—Clay was no-where, Polk wasn't thought of, Webster was but a patching, and Van Buren was small potatoes—the only comparisons to the returned representative, were Washington and old Hickory.

The signal was now given, and in poured the subscribers to the dinner, with their guest, and in poured John "on his own hook." The dining room shook with applause as the member took his seat. The judge presided upon the occasion, and after a blessing by the parson, they set to at the viands. We need not enter into particulars as to how the eatables looked or how they were eaten, suffice it they were choice and plentiful, and that the company showed an appreciatian of their worth by clearing the table! The host—on this occasion the happy host—stood behind the member's chair with a napkin, as if waiting for the great man to get through, so he might wipe his mouth and hands for him. The enthusiasm, and the liquor, had set the host's face in a glow; he looked as if he felt the greatness of the occasion, and he said he didn't care, if they devoured every thing in his house—he was repaid by the honor, indeed, he didn't know that he had anything more to live for after that day, it was the crowning period of his career. John, happy John! was actually devastating everything within his reach—he hadn't had such a chance for days, aye, weeks, and like Dugald Dalgetty, he not only made the most of the present, but carefully laid up a small provision for the future. He laughed at all jests within hearing, and scattered his own with unusual brilliancy.

The period had now arrived for the toasts and speeches, the feast of reason and the flow of liquor. After the regulars were drank, the county clerk gained the floor and offering a few striking and pertinent remarks, wherein he dwelt upon how the nation, and Indiana in particular, had been rescued by their representative, he proposed the following:

"Our representative, Charles Stumper, Esq., a pure patriot of Indiana, may a nation's gratitude yet make him a nation's head."

Amid the loud plaudits which followed, Charles Stumper, Esq., bowed his head as if that head was already a national crowning piece, and swallowing a spoonfull of cold water, he arose from his seat with a dignity befitting his august station. We have not room here to give his speech in detail—it was, of course, great—it couldn't be *anything else!* When he finished by saying that, "hereafter, body, bones, blood and all were devoted to their service," a shout went up that shook the town of M. like a small earthquake. Before he took his seat he offered the following compliment:

"The town of M., while its citizens have an existence, the country is safe!"

By a loud shout the citizens of M. proclaimed that they *would* save the country. During these enthusiastic proceedings our hero, by his urbanity, wit, sentiment, and good humor, had won a host of friends around him, and considerable curiosity was manifested to know who he was, but no one seemed able to give a satisfactory reply. Some said, he came with the congressman, and was his particular friend; others went so far as to intimate that he was another congressman in disguise—indeed, it was whispered that he was a senator *incog!*

"Hold on, fellars," said one of the citizens, "jest hold your hosses, boys—he'll come out directly; ther's suthin' more *in* that fellar than's on the outside!"

All appeared to agree to this sage opinion, and held their "hosses" accordingly. At length a pause occurring, as agreed upon by the editor of the county paper, the principal lawyer of the town toasted "The Press, the guardian of republican liberty." This toast was offered to afford the county editor a chance to deliver a speech, which he had prepared for the occasion, but before he could clear his throat and get upon his legs, John had gained the floor, and in a clear tone called the attention of the table. Here was a subject upon which John was at home—he knew the press "like a book," and with easy manner and consummate assurance, opened upon the great subject of its power. As he proceeded, all eyes dilated!—he pictured its progress from its earliest advent—its days of weakness, until its present wide-spread influence and power; he grew eloquent, and at length wound up with the following flourish:

"To the press, gentlemen, we owe all the astonishing achievements of modern times—they are the fruits of its power. It was the press which in an iron age unshackled the mind of man and gave free scope to his intellect,—taught him to soar over the elemental fields which gird him round about, and search into the sources of his own being, the causes which produced the great harmony in universal nature, and how to draw from those causes effects which would promote his happiness—sent him forth upon the great field of discovery, and spreading his achievements before the world, drew forth the might of mind to his aid, and now having led him to subdue the very lightning to his will, is by its aid scattering intelligence broadcast through the earth. It is not merely the guardian of Liberty—it is its creator!

As the sun is to the solar system, so is the press to human society; eclipse either, and man is left in a night of darkness more dreadful than annihilation!"

Applauses long and loud greeted his closing words; even the ladies, looking through the windows of the hotel from the porch which surrounded it, joined in the tokens of satisfaction, and now more eagerly than ever the question was propounded—"who is he?" No one knew, but all were high in his praise, and honors were showered so thick upon him that he hardly knew what he was about—every body wanted to drink with him, and he drank with every body. Order was called for his toast, and he gave—

"*The ladies of M.*—If heaven should blot out the stars, we will not discover the loss while surrounded by their bright eyes."

The huzzas became so deafening, the glory was so unexpected, and the liquor was so pungent, that John lost his compass, and began to beat about wild. Some one said he would make a first rate stump speaker, and to prove his capability he commenced a political speech, —sad mishap!—sad, because he forgot which side he should be on! and commenced a most scathing tirade against the very party he was feasting with. He had so won upon their good opinion that they listened patiently for awhile, but patience soon melted away, and "turn him out," was shouted from all sides of the table—the editor of the county paper was most violent for thrusting him out, for John had cut him out of his speech on the *press*.

"Turn him out!" shouted the editor, "he's a base *spy* in the camp.'

John perceived in a moment his fatal error, and felt happy that it did not occur until dinner was over—he felt that he had made an *impression*, and was proud that it was through no compromise of principle he had tasted of their hospitality, and showed them he was an opponent still; all that remained now, was to make a dignified retreat, and raising, with some difficulty, erect, he said:

"Gentlemen, when I entered, (hic)-tered this assembly, I thought I was among brethren, but I, (hic) I find I was deceived, and that I have been somewhat contaminated through error, so, (hic) so with your permission I'll withdraw and repent. I will no long-(hic) longer be one of you, but go forth to breathe a freer air."

At this moment he raised his hat to place it on his head, with a flourish, when out dropped the half of a *chicken*, and two *doughnuts*, which he had stowed away for a lunch. Their falling just at that particular moment bothered him, and to leave them there bothered him worse, but to pick them up was too humiliating—he scorned the action; since they would fall, why there let them lie, he would none of them.

"Old fellar," said a hoosier citizen, "you'd better pick up your chicken fixens afore you go."

"Never!" shouted John, indignantly, "I should des-(hic) despise myself if I carried off the spoils of the enemy—you and your fragments may go to the d——l!"

A yell followed his retreat, which would have shaken the nerves of a Coriolanus, but they steadied our hero's, and calm and composed he strode through the door lead ing from the dining room. The county editor seized the chicken and doughnuts, and hurled them after him, when John coolly closed the door, picked up the indignities, put them in his hat, and departed. Taking the road which led from the town, he turned his back upon the scene of the late festivities. As he again plodded onward he might be heard ejaculating—"Well, *wasn't* that a streak of *fat!* What a dinner! Fit for the gods, as I'm a gentleman! Rather funny at the winding up, but the commencement and the continuation was conducted with statesmanlike skill, and after all, the winding up was but an agreeable little interlude."

As John crept into a barn that night, some few miles from the town of M., and stretched himself upon the straw to sleep off the glories of the day, he quietly murmured to himself—"Well, here goes for another *streak of lean!*"

CHAPTER III.

JOHN'S EDITORIAL CAREER.

In our hero's peregrinations he wandered into the Sucker state, the country of vast projected rail roads, good corndodger, splendid banking houses, and poor currency, and during his progress therein he earned and hoarded about one hundred and fifty bona fide dollars. With this store of wealth jingling in his pockets, he entered the town of B——; he did not come now as the needy adventurer, but as one holding one hundred and fifty considerations entitling him to respect. The world had taken a wider spread to his eye, and assumed new features, or rather he began to see with a clearer vision, for the common order of society appeared now, as plain as daylight, to have most villainous faces, and the *respectability* of wealth was as apparent as moonshine—he could now easily assign a reason for the deference paid to high station—in short, he had arrived at a state of feeling highly becoming the possessor of increasing wealth. Addressing the innkeeper of the town, who was a member of one of the *first* families, with an air of consequence, he demanded a whole room for his accommodation, when heretofore the third chance in a bed would have been considered a luxury, oriental in its character, and a blessing befitting a "three tailed bashaw."

The little town was an important one, as all sucker towns are, yet the arrival of our hero was enough to create a sensation from its one extremity to the other. An acquaintance with the innkeeper soon gained him an introduction to the member of the legislature from that district, and this opening soon made him intimate with the town. Many efforts were made by the citizens to "draw him out," and learn his business, but John kept dark. "He's a close fellar," said a sucker citizen, "but I reckon, arter all, his business is pole-ticks." These and sundry other "ambiguous givings out," assured our hero that he was a subject of general interest. "What is his politics?" was a question of import, duly discussed in the leading political circles; and "was he married?"—and, "who'd get him, if he wasn't?" was equally an absorbing matter of interest among the ladies; indeed, an animated discussion as to his preference had already caused a coolness between several pairs of devoted female friends. It was said that the pert Miss A—, the storekeeper's daughter, had absolutely walked down the principal street of B——, right before our hero, swinging the skirt of her frock in a most enticing manner. Such a bold and forced movement to take him by surprise, before any other maid could get a chance, was declared, at a tea and gossip party, to be most "tolerable and not to be endured." At length his object was made known—he inquired of the legislative member, if that was a good point to establish a paper, and as soon as his surprise would permit, the member declared it to be an *immense* place, indeed, an *enormous* location, and more than that, the material for an establishment was in the town, had been in operation, and all it wanted was an editor to conduct the paper. John signified his ability and willingness, and the intelligence spread through the town like a prairie fire, and some pretty noses turned up as their owners exclaimed—"Why, I swow, he's only a printer, after all!"

The member for the district, a long, lanky, cadaverous lawyer, who was death on a speech, powerful in chewing tobacco, and some at a whisky drinking, was part owner of the printing concern, and having an opponent in the district, who had started a paper in the lower town, on the river, to oppose him, he was most anxious to get the press going; so, assuring John he could have it at his own terms, and one hundred and fifty subscribers to commence with, which must of course swell to a thousand, they settled the matter, and proceeded to examine the establishment. It was at length agreed that our hero should give one hundred and twenty-five dollars of his one hundred and fifty, in cash, and his note for four hundred and fifty dollars more, payable at the end of a year, besides fifty dollars rent for the office, which also belonged to the lawyer. A meeting of the *first* citizens of the town was held on the ensuing evening, to which John Earl, Esq., was formally introduced as the new editor of the B—— Eagle, and the re-commencement of the paper duly discussed.

"You've hearn tell of the bank and tariff questions?" inquired a leading constituent and subscriber.

John answered "yes," he was somewhat acquainted with them.

"Well, hoss, we 'spect you to be right co-chunk up to the hub on them thar questions, and to pour it inter the inimy in slashergaff style."

John agreed to do his prettiest.

"In the town below us," continued the constituent, "thar is a fellar of the inimy who's dead bitter agin us and our town, so you must gin him scissors! Rile him up, and sot his liver workin', 'cause the skunk is injurin' our location. Advartis' our doins' in gineral, sich as we got to sell, and throw yourself wide on the literary fixins and poetry, for the galls—*and*, Mister Earl, ef you ony do this genteely, and with spirit, the whole town will *take the paper!* Don't forgit to gin the town below particular saltpetre."

John gave them to understand that if his subscribers wished it, he would not only cut up the editor, but throw the lower town into a series of fits which would cause its utter dissolution. All being duly settled, our hero retired to his room to dream of future greatness. Already did he behold sheets filled with editorial tact and talent—already was his name inscribed upon the roll with illustrious editorial contemporaries—Ritchie,

Pleasants, Blair, Gales, Chandler, Prentice and Neal, those great names of the tripod tribe already numbered him on their list, and he fancied "his name grown great in mouths of wisest censure," while his pockets were correspondingly corpulent with the reward for such ability. Poor fellow, could he have drawn aside the curtain, and beheld the days of toil, the struggles to procure ink and paper, the labor of writing editorials, and the labor of setting them up, working them off at press, pasting up the mail, and the lack of reward which repaid this drudgery, he would have kicked ambition out of his company, and clutched his little hoard like a vice.

The town of B—— and the town below, had been rivals ever since they were first laid out upon a map—the growth of one had always been the envy of the other, and an improvement in one was sure to be imitated by the other. The lower town had been most successful in the publication of a newspaper, for the reason that they *paid something* to support it, while the town of B—— suffered for the neglect they manifested towards the press. The editor below not only abused the religion, politics, merchandise, and intelligence of B——, but the beauty of the women, and the smartness of the babies; he had even gone so far as to say that B—— women and babies could be known by their heads. This was an outrage most unpardonable, and John rose in estimation as their defender against such vandal accusations.

Behold John seated scratching out his *first* editorial! Ah, ye weavers of cheap literature, who have watched with aching curiosity the appearance of your first production—ye writers of small poetry for daily journals, who have listened so eagerly for praise—ye penny editors who have successfully tickled the popular ear—ye ruling deities of mammoth weeklies, what are all your feelings, concentrated into one great throb, in comparison to the mighty throes of talent waking from her sleep in the mind of John Earl. It would have shocked the lower town like the heaving of a volcano, had they but known the shower of expletives our hero was tracing on the sheet before him. Goths and Vandals, corruption and spoilsmen, traitors and apostates, vile incendiaries and polluting vipers, poisonous demagogues, and a host more, bitter as sin, were showered like hail from his pen, when giving "perticular goss" to the lower town editor and his abettors.

With the appearance of the first number our hero's consequence began to rise, the *respectable* citizens took him cordially by the hand, and their daughters smiled upon him, while the *poorer* inhabitants wondered at his "larnin'."

"A most excellent first number," said the lanky member, "a good quantity of hot shot—just the thing—sew the lower town up—you've got prodigious talents—immense!"

John bowed to the pleasing flattery.

"Well, hoss," said the storekeeper constituent and subscriber, "You've slashed the hide off'er that fellar in the lower town, touched his raw, and rumpled his feathers—that's the way to give him jessy. I raily believe you'll git yourself inter the legislatur' afore long, ef you keep on."

Our hero listened to these first breathings of fame

with a swelling bosom—there was a chance of his becoming somebody, at last, and labor became a pleasure when it produced such a yield. At a public meeting called in the town he was elected secretary, and ventured on the occasion to make a speech, which was loudly applauded, and in the next number of the Eagle appeared a glowing description of the proceedings, with a synopsis of his own speech. This awoke some jealousy in the mind of the lanky member, who thought John wished to supplant him. As time progressed the Eagle increased its subscription to two hundred, its editor grew popular, in debt, and received nothing from his subscribers—indeed, he soon discovered that pay made up no part of their patronage, and he began to grow tired of laboring for glory alone. All this time the war was waging hotter and thicker between the towns and their editors. At length he of the lower town inserted in his "Patriotic Herald and Telegraph" the following:

☞"We are informed, from good authority, that the *Buzzard* of the *Eagle* cannot pay his board bill, and fears are entertained that he will *slope* without liquidating the debt!"

This was personal—every body said it was personal—the lanky member said it must be wiped out with *blood*—the storekeeper swore that John must "eat the other fellar's *gizzard*," and the ladies of B—— resolved, at a tea party, that the death of the lower town editor could alone atone for the many indignities he had heaped upon them, and John was the very man to offer himself up as a sacrifice. All the subscribers to the Eagle were interested in the matter, for they would gain in any event, as how: If the lower town editor was removed, an enemy had perished; if John fell, a creditor's accounts were closed, so they were unanimous for a duel. The lanky member informed John of the general opinion of the public as to what he should do, and urged the sending of a challenge forthwith, which he offered to bear. John intimated that he must have a day to practise before he sent the missive, and this was acceded to as prudent, but bowie knives were recommended by his friend as much the *safest* and sure means of killing.

Our hero seated himself in the Eagle office that night, where the ghost of his departed greatness visited his waking thoughts, to laugh at his present misery. Of his one hundred and fifty dollars, but twenty-five remained—his clothes were nearly worn out—his board bill unpaid—his subscriptions and advertisements ditto, and the supply of paper and ink was insufficient for another issue, besides a duel on hand with another poor devil of an editor, and the whole town thirsting for the bloody transaction. A thought flashed upon his brain—he would go see his antagonist. No sooner was the idea conceived than he put it in execution. Gathering up his remaining twenty-five dollars he set off in the night for the lower town, where he arrived about daylight. After a hasty breakfast at the inn, he entered the "Herald office," and seating himself upon the only chair in the establishment, inquired for the editor. A little pale man, engaged at *case*, lay down his composing *stick* and advanced, expecting a new subscriber, but started to run as soon as he was informed that the editor of the "Eagle" was before him. John stopped his egress and made him sit down while he talked to him. A conversation brought on mutual apologies, and he found his antagonist as great a sufferer as himself—the mere hack of county politicians, who had been lured by the same phantom—greatness, until he had worn himself to a corresponding shadow, chasing the vision. The two typo editors shook hands in friendship, and our hero departed homeward.

On John's arrival he encountered the member, who urged the immediate despatch of the challenge, which John refused, and to his refusal added some words of contempt for the citizens of B——, and their representative in particular. This aroused the member, who declared that *cowardice* had driven him over to the enemy. To prove the falsehood of this assertion, John knocked the member down, and kicked his honor must indignantly. The editor of the Eagle was well aware, that after this outbreak he must "break for tall timber," so cooking a smash dish of *pi* in his office, he bequeathed the feast to his successor, and leaving his subscription list, and interest in the concern, to pay his debts, he beat a hasty retreat. As he hurried through the woods skirting the river, the welcome puff of a steamer saluted his ear, and waving his handkerchief as a signal, she stopped, landed a boat, and took him on board.

Farewell to B——, its dreams of greatness had faded to mist, and instead of growing honor, emolument, and renown, it had yielded naught but the fruit of bitterness, accompanied with toil and care, the end of which was a roll back to the bottom of the hill he had fancied already climbed. The great of earth will smile at his troubles, —happy for him that his disposition would only permit them to cause a momentary sadness. As the steamer receded from the scene of his late vexation and care, he began to rejoice in his freedom, and in a light-hearted mood paced her deck, an untrammelled candidate for new fortune. Bright dreams of the future came again, and what a blessing it is that the lonely adventurer in this world is permitted to dream, for with a vivid imagination he may revel in joys which waking reality can never equal.

Let us return a moment to B——. All there, as may be supposed, was a scene of confusion, indignation, and horror, at the outrage inflicted upon the member—he had absolutely been *kicked!* A warrant was issued for John, and then it was discovered *he* had *sloped*—more indignation! The editor of the lower town still lived, and the member had been kicked—horror! The office of the Eagle was in *pi* and its editor *non est*, which means nowhere—terrible excitement! Here was capital for the lower town editor, and didn't he use it—to use a classical expression he *lit* upon the upper town and its member "like a thousand of brick!" He charged them with starving their editor, charged their editor with cowardice, charged the member with tamely submitting to be kicked by the aforesaid cowardly editor, and wound up by asserting that the town of B—— produced nothing but pusillanimous men, ugly women, and pug-nosed babies! The glory of B——, departed while the lower town swelled into vast importance, and its editor received a present of *two* new shirts from the ladies of his section, besides three spirited subscribers paid him one dollar each, of their four years subscription—a stretch of liberality so astounding, that to this day the event forms one of the most interesting legends of the Sucker state.

CHAPTER IV.

HIS WANDERINGS THROUGH THE PRAIRIES.

John, now released from his thraldom, bent his way to Chicago, to pursue fortune in the lake country, and landing at Peoria, he resolved to foot it across the prairies, to the head of Lake Michigan. His store, as usual, embraced a scanty wardrobe, attached to the end of a stick, and twenty dollars in cash. As he journeyed on, he would occasionally break into a laugh as the recollections of B—— would intrude themselves upon his thoughts. His former castle-building, however, served to enliven the way with merriment, as foot and eye travelled into the future, and setting the past down as so much paid for experience, he consoled himself with the thought of his youth and health, snapped his fingers at care, and held himself in an easy state of mind to receive whatever fate might send him. At the close of the second day of his journey he halted on the edge of a prairie at a small log house. A tidy woman was bustling about in the interior, and two children, whose little faces were yellow as saffron, sat listlessly upon the door sill, playing with bits of broken delf. Their narrow habitation presented little of comfort to cheer the inmates or welcome the traveller. He inquired if he could lodge there, and the woman answered that such as she had to offer, he was welcome to, but being a lonely widow, and far from where any thing comfortable could be obtained, she had but poor accommodations to offer. Our hero was easily pleased, and so signified to her. Depositing his bundle within, he took the axe from her hands, with which she was about to chop some wood, and throwing off his coat, he prepared the fuel to cook their evening repast, then seating himself upon a hickory bottomed chair, he took the widow's sickly little daughter upon his knee, and coaxed a smile into her wan countenance. The mother watched the gambols of her child with the merry stranger, and a tear of pleasure sparkled in her eye, while the feeling sent a pleasing expression over her sad countenance; she spoke to him, too, in a tone of kindness different from her first words, because there was something friendly about his manner, and his light-hearted gayety was cheering to her sorrow.

When the table was spread, the corn cakes and pork placed upon it, with some milk, John seated himself with the children beside him, and attended to their little wants, with such kindness of manner, that ere the meal had ended, the little family began to imbibe something of their guest's gay spirit. As they gathered around the fire that evening, the widow ventured to inquire where her visiter was from, and when he informed her he was a Philadelphian, her eyes filled with tears,—that, too, was her birthplace. Looking upon the stranger, now, as a brother whom she had encountered in the wilderness, she poured into his ear her sad story. Her husband and herself, both young, had started some years previous from Philadelphia, for the west—his object being to secure a home of his own, and liking the spot where their cabin stood, they "squatted;" all went cheerfully for a time, but sickness soon came, and the prevailing fever of the country had swept him away from her side, leaving her far from the home of her childhood, with two children, friendless and alone. Sad days had passed since then, and hope was almost dead within her. Beneath a small hillock, surrounded with a little paling of pointed sticks, drove into the ground by her own hands, reposed the remains of her husband, and there lay buried all her hopes for the future. John spoke cheeringly to her, and to divert her thoughts from present sorrow, talked of their far-off home. The widow's little girl nestled in his lap, her little hands clasped around one of his, her head reclining upon his breast, while on a stool at the mother's side sat her little boy, and thus and there the wandering printer called up a panorama of their birthplace. Old Christ Church bells sounded in their ears again a Christmas' peal—together they wandered by the Schuylkill side; or, climbing Fair Mount hill, looked out upon the wide-spread city; or, trod again its streets teeming with a gay and busy populace—each well-known antique habitation or hall, remembered by both, was spoken of with affection, as a memento of happy days—the wide and dreary prairie, over which the autumn wind was sighing cold and sadly, was forgotten now—scenes far away rose like shadows around the inhabitants of the log mansion, and the hum of the old city drowned the voice of the west wind, as it moaned around their dwelling. There was the place, and those the circumstances, in which home wore its most heavenly hue. The lone widow that night thanked Heaven in her prayers, that one had been directed across her pathway to cheer her heart with sweet remembrances; and in her dreams, as she wandered again among the scenes of childhood, the faces she met all bore resemblance to the stranger—their tones of welcome sounded like his, and a smile, sweet as ever, rested upon a virtuous mother's lip; she slumbered through the live long night in happiness. The good angel, who registers kindness of mortal to mortal, surely marked here a credit in favor of the typo.

When the morning sun cast his golden sheen over the rich carpet of the prairie, John prepared to depart, and shaking the widow by the hand, he assured her that she should see home again, for he would search out her friends and have her sent for. As he stepped off from the house, the little girl run after him for a farewell kiss, and taking out of his pocket the remainder of his little wealth, seventeen dollars in all, he reserved one dollar for his travelling expenses, and placing his purse, with the remaining sixteen dollars, in the belt of the child, sent her back to her mother, and with the step of an emperor strode on his way. At the brow of a rising slope, in view of the cabin, he turned back to look, and saw the widow and her little ones watching his receding footsteps—raising his hat and kissing his hand he turned down the slope and was soon hidden from their sight. *Improvident* John, to thus give all thy store, except a trifle, to the widow and the orphan. Ah, ye cold and sordid ones of earth, a single thrill such as played about his heart then, was worth a mountain of your money bags. Contrasting his situation with the poor widow whom he had just departed from, he felt rich as Crœsus—the craft of his hand, his robust youth, and a single dollar were odds in his favor against the worst circumstances.

Two days more had passed when weary and foot-sore he approached a small village, and accosting an inhabitant leaning over a fence, he inquired if there was any chance of employment in the neighborhood.

"Well, I'm of the opinion, stranger," said the sucker, "that your chance here, is pretty much as to what you can do—ef you'r anythin' of a brick maker, Old Jo Simms wants a man at his yard, down thar at the branch; but you don't look amazin' like a mud moulder, hoss!"

"I'm not much for looks," said John, "but I'm creation at shaping things, and as for bricks, I'm a whole load of them—'front stretchers,' at that—made of choice clay—Father Adam's patent—so just point the way to Jo Simms, and some day come over and see a specimen of my brick."

Receiving the proper direction, down he went to the brick-maker's dwelling, where, on entering, he encountered old Mrs. Jo Simms, and a look at her good humored countenance satisfied him, that an instalment on his new situation, in the shape of a supper and bed, was not only possible, but very probable. After making known his business, the old lady surveyed his person, and remarked—

"Well, the old man did talk of hirin' some help, 'cause thar's a lot of brick orders on hand, and I suppose you mought do—you look dreadful draggled though, and tired as a prairie team, arter a hard day's ploughin'."

John readily assented to her comment on his appearance, and asked if he could'nt have something to eat and a bed, for he was both tired and hungry, after his tramp to see about the situation. The good matron, sympathisingly, prepared him a good supper, and conducted him to a small, neat room over the kitchen, where a clean bed and comfortable covering lay temptingly in repose, as if waiting for some weary body, to rest it. This was no time to philosophise on luck, so John turned in and straight addressed himself to sleep—it came without coaxing, and as Morpheus wrapped him in her poppy robe, it seemed to him a covering of the softest fur and brightest hues. His dreams were peopled by a weary train of foot passengers, who toiled along beneath a burning sun, with sticks across their shoulders, and bundles dangling at their ends, while *he* seemed drawn on a chariot of air, whose delightful floating motion lulled the senses into a soft, dreamy languor—not a sleep of forgetfulness, but one where the brain was sensible of the body's enjoyment—and refreshing breezes, laden with the fragrance of prairie flowers, fanned his brow. It was mortality tasting the repose of the gods! When morning broke John turned himself on his couch just to realise the truth of his situation, and hugged the covering to his rested body with a lover's fervor. As he thus lay enjoying the waking reality, a conversation in the kitchen below him attracted his attention. The old lady was telling her son, a young man, that an applicant for the situation of help in the yard, was sleeping above.

"What, have you engaged him?" inquired the son.

"No, not azactly engaged him, but I gin the poor creatur' suthin' to eat, and sent him to bed, expectin' to be engaged in the mornin'—he's not jest strong enough, but appears mity willin'."

"Well, I'm consarned sorry you did any sich a thing," said he, "'cause we won't want a man for a month yit."

"Well, the creatur' *will* be dreadfully disappinted," answered the old lady.

"Not so much as you think, Mrs. Jo Simms," thought our hero, and then he began to congratulate himself on his good fortune:

"I am a most lucky disciple of Faust," said he, "I've had a supper fit for a lord, and a couch where the imperial form of sovereignty might repose unruffled —and did—for I'm an august representative of American sovereignty! What next? If the good angel of the lonely widow and her little ones don't now desert me, I stand 'a right smart chance' of getting a breakfast into the bargain!—Well," concluded John, "this is too much luck for weak human nature to bear easily, so it is necessary to nerve myself, or I shall be overcome." Dressing himself, he descended to the kitchen, and made the acquaintance of the younger Jo Simms, who appeared very backward in breaking to our hero the sad news of his rejection as help in the yard. At length, however, he kindly broke the intelligence, and before John could answer he offered him two dollars to pay his expenses back, and, moreover, invited him to partake of the smoking repast just preparing.

"Say no more about it, my dear sir," says John, "such liberality removes the pain of disappointment."

It was refreshing to see how his phiz lighted up at his luck, and all parties being perfectly satisfied, they enjoyed the morning meal with a relish. As John was about to depart, the good old dame rolled him up a lunch of short cake, and he bid farewell to brick making.

In a short time he arrived at Chicago, where he obtained work at his business, but the exposure he had undergone brought on the fever and ague, which shook him out of all respect for Illinois, and he therefore determined to leave it, so embarking one bright morning, he shook it an adieu which made his teeth chatter, which excitement was of course followed by a most subduing fever.

On the fifth day after their departure from Chicago, while crossing the head of Lake Erie, from Detroit river towards Cleveland, John had stretched himself after a shake, upon a settee at the head of the cabin, and in sight of the gangway leading to the boiler deck, and while thus in a reposing attitude he was enjoying quietly his fever, he observed one of the hands ascend from below, his visage all begrimed and covered with a profuse perspiration, and cautiously approach the captain, to whom he whispered something which produced much excitement in the commander's countenance, but his manner exhibited no haste. Coolly walking through the cabin and around the boat, he approached the gangway and looked below, then carefully surveyed the passengers, as if to note whether he was observed. John, who had been watching his movements, arose from his couch and advanced towards him, the captain spread himself before the hold to prevent his seeing below, whereupon our hero, who had shrewdly guessed the cause of his agitation, whispered in his ear to descend, that he knew the steamer was on *fire* below, and while endeavouring to quench it, he would divert the attention of any who might approach the hold. The captain thanked him, and John took his post. How dreadful was their situation, yet how unconcerned all on board walked about, or lounged upon seats around the cabin and decks. Beneath them struggled one destroying element, and around them on either side, dancing in the sunbeams, spread another; while like a thread upon the surface of the far-off waters appeared the only land in view. Oh, how the flickering flame struggled in that dark hold for mastery, and how bravely the sinewy arms of its late masters battled to get it again in bondage. At one moment the hissing water appeared to have quenched it, but the next the bright flame curled up far in by the boiler side, and a fold of dark smoke would roll out derisively in the face of its foes. It was a contest for life, and here upon the broad wave the fire had them at fearful odds. In a short time the commander appeared on deck, very much agitated, and taking our hero aside, he declared to him that there was no hope—the fire was increasing! Calling the passengers together, he informed them of their situation, and opening a closet distributed among them a number of life preservers, then ordering the boats cleared, he coolly prepared for the catastrophe. Some of the passengers grew almost frantic; and if not prevented, would have plunged overboard to certain death; others calmly prepared for the worst, and some were amusing in their lamentations.

"Captin, you'll hev tu pay right smartly for that truck of mine, if you git it spiled," said a down easter, "and it's jest my luck tu meet with sech consarned ruin.—There ain't no sea sarpints in this lake as you know on, is there? du tell us, now, afore a fellow's shoved off."

"Is it sarpents?" inquired an Irishman, "oh, me darlint, if that was all we had to contind with, I'd curl him up like the worm uv a still, wid the crass I've got, but it's the thunderin' sharks that'll make short work uv a body, and divil a crass'll pravint thim."

"Now, these things," said Jonathan, holding up a gum elastic, "they calls life presarvers; why, I swow tu gracious, if they aint more like patent forks, tu hold a fellar up, while the consarned lake varmints nibbles his legs off, comfortably."

A large fat lady, who had provided herself with an enormous sized preserver, was in a dreadful way to know if her chance for floating was at all probable.

"Why, bless you, Marm," said the mate, "there's wind enough about you to float a whaler."—The fat lady became tranquil with this assurance.

It was now proposed by the captain, to cut a hole through the vessel's deck, and pour in water directly upon the fire; this being the only hope for saving the vessel, it was instantly adopted, and willing hands in a few moments made the opening, into which the boat's hose was turned, and in a brief period, the engineer reported the heat abating. The spirits of all on board revived on hearing this intelligence, and a further application of the counter element removed all grounds for fear. As the horrors of their late situation disappeared, the light house at the mouth of Cleveland harbor rose in view, calming the fears of all, and marking in its welcome proportions the scene of rest for our wandering hero. What here chanced to befall him we shall reserve for our concluding chapter.

CHAPTER V.

HIS ENCOUNTER WITH OLD FRIENDS.

Our hero, on landing in Cleveland, placed his bundle in one hand, and stick in the other, and thus leisurely sauntered up the hill and through the main street of this young mart of trade. Although his body drooped with sickness, the air of life and thriving industry which surrounded him, aroused his active mind to exertion. His old companion of travel resided here, and now was a fitting time to try his professions of regard. While reading the signs along the street, he mentally ventured the opinion that "Smith & Co." were doing an extensive business, for their name was attached to commercial concerns all over the country ; and as thus ruminating, another, and quite as familiar a name, met his eye, besides it was a vastly more interesting name—none other than his old adopted *Father's* cognomen. He could scarcely bring himself to believe that the imposing store before him was really occupied by those who were so endeared to him by past kindness—that was a streak of too good luck to be possible ; nevertheless, thinking he might gratify himself with a peep at the possessor of so honored a name, he approached the window, and looked into the interior—can it be ?—yes it is !—"plain as a pipe stem"—sure enough, his old adopted father stood before him ! There, amid the piles of soles and uppers, with spectacles on nose, and head a little bald, stood that veritable good old *soul*, who had sheltered his infant years. Time had not furrowed his brow with the chisel, but his brush had traced its easy progress; nor had the storm torn away his locks—the gentle zephyr had plucked the silvery threads away to sport with them in the sunbeam. Contentment lingered in his quiet smile, and "well to do in the world," was legibly written upon his portly person. John entered the store, and putting on the air of a purchaser, seated himself upon a settee, and held his foot up to be measured—the old man adjusted his spectacles, kneeled down upon one knee, stole a glance over his glasses at his customer, and commenced taking the dimensions of our hero's foot; but there was an indescribable something about the face, which drove the foot from his memory, and while he was trying to rake up from the past some known body on which to fix the head and face, he forgot that he was holding the foot, until John asked him, if "there was anything uncommon about its shape?" The old man, stammering an excuse, started to his drawers to select a pair of the right size, but the stranger's face again so mixed itself up with the figures on his strap and rule, that he was forced to return and measure the foot over again. John observed his quandary, and smiled at the old man's efforts to recollect him. At this moment the old lady came to the door separating the shop from the dwelling, and looking in, spoke to her husband; our hero recognised her in a moment, he could not refrain himself, but springing to his feet with a shout, he laughingly held out his arms, exclaiming "Mother, don't you know me!" If not at the first glance, the tones of his voice, and the ring of his merry laughter, called up the vivid remembrance of his boyish days with the rapidity of thought, and throwing herself into his arms she sobbed with joy, as if he were in verity her own long lost offspring; the old man, too, dropping his measure, seized our hero; and here tears of true feeling mingled in one current—remembrances of the past clustered around, and joy, deep and holy as dwells within the human breast, held uninterrupted revel.

The store was closed early that night, and as they were seated round the evening meal, John would, with sketches of his past history since they parted, at one moment draw from them shouts of merriment, and then again, as he dwelt on some hard streak of fortune, "beguile them of their tears." Oh, it was a happy night, that night of meeting on the shore of the broad lake. The gay revel within sumptuous halls affords no joy like this, for here the fountains of the heart danced to the music of affection; the air to which they kept time was "past days," and their pure current swelled into a flood of nature's kindliest harmony—all was joy, all happiness. With a motherly care, as in days of his childhood, the old lady stripped his neck, and washed away the dust of travel, then conducting him to a neatly furnished chamber, she kissed him good night, and retired to thank Heaven that her aged eyes had been permitted to see him again. While our hero slept happily above, the old folks talked long and earnestly in the chamber beneath him, and before they closed their eyes in sleep, resolved that he should never again part from them. They had none in this world to care for, save him, and Heaven, the old lady said, had sent him back to their roof to be an honor and comfort to their old age. In the morning they awoke to a renewal of these happy feelings, and over the breakfast table future plans were freely discussed. John mentioned his travelling acquaintance, and taking the card from his vest pocket, showed it to his adopted father, who immediately recognised the owner as one of his customers, one of the most wealthy, and of course, respected citizens in Cleveland. To visit him a new suit was necessary, and after the morning meal the old man piloted him to a tailoring establishment, and fitted him from head to foot in a fine suit—in short, he disguised our hero, and it was pleasant to see with what admiration the aged couple looked through their spectacles at the change.

"I *de*-clare if you don't look like a gentleman, when you're dressed," said the old lady.

"And why not, mother?" inquired John." It is the material which passes current for gentility. If half mankind, who now move through good society unquestioned, were placed in my old dusty suit, the world would never discover their claims to the title—no, no! After all, your fine suit is the world's standard of a fine gentleman—it will gain the owner consideration among mixed assemblies—credit in the mart of trade—a high place in the synagogue, and moreover, it is a general ticket, entitling its possessor to the world's civility!"

"Well, bless me!" exclaimed the old woman, "if they don't make a change in your talk—you're gittin' right toploftical."

After many thanks on our hero's part, and much admiration on the part of his friends, he received permission to wander forth and see his old friend of the *road*, to whose dwelling he was correctly directed by the shoe dealer. A kiss from his adopted mother, a five dollar bill from the old man, for pocket money, and out sallied John, his person erect, and step buoyant with good fortune—sickness had almost fled before his revived hopes.

The aged pair stood in the store door gazing on his

manly form, as he receded from them, and a feeling of pride glowed in their hearts, the nearest akin to a parent's, that nature will permit. They knew that no one could rightfully dispute their claim to him, and proud in their pre-emption right, they retired into their dwelling with newly awakened pleasure. Arrived at his travelling acquaintance's mansion, he looked at the name of "Charles C. Briggs, Attorney at Law," upon the door plate, and a glance at the exterior of the building, assured him that the dweller therein was one of the prosperous class of his profession. Knocking at the office door in the basement, he was bid enter, and on doing so found seated at a desk, surrounded with piles of legal lore, the same old gentleman who had so kindly bid him farewell at Wheeling. The recognition was mutual, and the old man's manner truly cordial.

"So, you found me out," said the attorney.

"Yes," replied John, "but a precious long tramp I've had to reach you."

His friend insisted upon his seating himself, and relating an outline of his adventures, at which he laughed most heartily, and when John had finished, he clapped him on the back, saying—

"You are a lucky dog—in your first journey you have gathered more lessons of wisdom, than many meet with in a life time, and your mind may turn them into vast profit."

"Well, I'd like to realise something out of them," quietly remarked our hero, "for I have expended all my capital in learning them."

"And so, you have found other friends besides myself in Cleveland," remarked the lawyer, "a worthy couple whom I happen to be acquainted with, also;

between us, I think we will persuade you to become a fixture of society. I know not why, but I like you, and have often wished for the present meeting. Having no son of my own to assist me in my old days, and continue my business after me, I have felt a desire to find one who would fill the vacancy; your intelligence and happy disposition, on our trip, made me like you, and now I would fain ripen those feelings into a strong bond of friendship. Come, you must dine with me, and then we will talk of the future."

John's heart was swelling with friendship already, and he could almost have hugged the kind old lawyer, but as this was his first day at his adopted parents, he was forced to excuse himself for the present, on promise of returning on the morrow, and with kindling aspirations and noble resolves, he returned to his parents. There he recounted the lawyer's words, and made known his intention of studying law with him, which met with general approval, and the little household put on quite an air of importance about its acquisition, while its mistress hurried about, chatting with her new found child with all the garrulousness of kindly old age.

On the next day, John, according to appointment, placed his legs under the mahogany of his friend, the lawyer, and while the meal progressed he amused the company by relating some episodes of his travel and observation, but every now and then, a strange quietness might be observed to pass over his demeanor, and his eyes would wander furtively to the other end of the table, where was seated the fair daughter of his host, whose dark eyes met his stolen glances, and sent the blood tingling to his brows. Look another way, John, —there's danger in those dark eyes! What, you, who have looked unmoved at scores of bright eyes, to tremble now at a single pair—out upon you—look straight into those dark orbs, and dare their power—now!—pshaw, man, you shake and stammer as if a battery of loaded cannon, with the lighted fusees behind them, were pointed at you. Ah, I see, your merriment is at an end now—busy thoughts, strange dreams, and bright hopes are coursing through your bewildered brain. And so they were—that visit had planted new feelings in his breast. He entered the old lawyer's mansion, as he thought, the possessor of all he wished on earth—a home, and an opportunity to rise—yet here was aroused a feeling which absorbed all the rest—he never felt himself poor before. Before, he was the possessor of a light heart, but now that heart had been spirited away by a felonious pair of eyes, and his mind was racked with dread, for fear he might not be able to compromise with the possessor, and be permitted to keep it company—here was a "*take*" in the book of human nature, which was most "fair copy," and fain would our hero take unto himself the *page*. Fear not, John, all in good time—the fair daughter of your old friend is troubled, too—a merry printer has, by his gentle manners, and most winning address, made a deep *impression* there, and is sadly troubling the little heart of its fair possessor. She thinks, she would like to forget him, but in trying to do so she must think of what she would forget, and thus he ever comes uppermost in her mind, and his pleasing countenance and coaxing eye gains a firmer footing in her affections.

Arrangements were made before the lawyer and our hero parted, that he should forthwith commence the study of law, and accordingly he set himself down *upon* [illegible] Coke and Littleton, with the determination of becoming a pillar of the state. A most dangerous neighborhood he chose to study in—dangerous for the hasty progress of his studies in legal lore, for long before he was fitted for a single degree, as a *student* at the bar, he had become a *professor* of love; and how soon he learned to look deep into those eyes, and read the mind within, twine himself around the tendrils of the fair girl's heart, and plead in choicest language for permission to nestle there; and how the eyes softly permitted the bold student to look, and then loved to have him look, and, then consented that he might gaze at will—aye, *for life!*

On a clear wintry night, while the wind of the lake whistled merrily across its congealed bosom, and the stars were looking down with clear faces into the bright icy mirror beneath—the sound of sweet music, and the tread of light feet resounded in the mansion of the old lawyer, by the broad lake side,—a "merrie companie" filled its halls, for John Earl, the no longer "wandering typo," was about to become his son-in-law—or, son-in-love, as well as law—or both—and the bright eyes of one of Ohio's fairest daughters looked all confidingness and love, as she stood up before the assembled throng, and whispered herself into his possession. There was gay doings that night in this western mansion, and joy that age was a large partaker of; for the old pair, who sheltered the printer's orphan, years agone, and miles away, were guests within it, and their hearts swelled with pride, as they looked upon their adopted child, and his fair bride. The old shoemaker quietly remarked to his happy son, that no maid in the city stepped upon a more fairy foot, or wore so small a shoe; but he hoped to live long enough, to make a smaller size for the Earl family, and then he laughed as if the job would be a right merry one, and the purchaser of such a shoe, a favored customer.

Time has progressed since then, and we have listened to John Earl, Esq., in the capital of his adopted state, as in clear tones, and patriotic fervor, he stood advocating the great truths of republican principles, and we have listened with pride and admiration, when those words proved that the child of the people, was the people's advocate. He did not, in his hour of prosperity, forget the lonely widow of the prairie, but had her and her little ones brought to Cleveland, and having by letters found her friends, he sent her home rejoicing—the little one to whom he last bid adieu in the wilderness still remembered him, and with her little lips pouting for a kiss, was the last again to bid him farewell.

We have traced our hero to the end of his wanderings, and leave him upon the stage of public action—on the road to eminence; and though many may read as though these words and scenes were the coinage of the writer's brain, yet let him assure those who so judge, that there be such "streaks of life," in the book of a Typo's biography.

"NOT A DROP MORE, MAJOR, UNLESS IT'S SWEETEN'D."

In a small village, in the southern section of Missouri, resides a certain Major, who keeps a small, *cosey*, comfortable little inn, famous for its *sweeten'd drinks*, as well as jovial landlord; and few of the surrounding farmers visit the neighborhood, without giving the Major a friendly call, to taste his *mixtur'*. The gay host, with jolly phiz, round person, bright eye, and military air, deals out the rations, spiced with jokes, which, if they are not funny, are at least laughed at, for the Major enjoys them so vastly himself, that his auditors are forced to laugh, out of pure sympathy.

A good old couple, who resided about six miles from the Major's, for a long period had been in the habit of visiting him once a month, and as regularly went home dreadfully *sweeten'd* with the favorite *mixtur'*; but of late, we learn, the amicable relations existing between the Major and his old visitors have been broken off by green-eyed jealousy. On the last visit, good cause was given for an end being put to any more "sweet drinking."

"Uncle Merril, how *are* you, *any* how," was the Major's greeting, "and I *de*clare if the Missus aint with you, *too*"—just as if he expected she wouldn't come. "What'll you take Missus? shall I *sweeten* you a little of about *the* best Cincinnati rectified that ever was *toted* into these 'ere parts?—it jest looks as bright as your eyes!" and here the Major winked and looked so sweet there was no resisting, and she *did* take a little sweeten'd.

The hours flew *merril*-ly by, and evening found the old couple so overloaded with sweets, that it was with great difficulty they could be seated on the old grey mare, to return home; but, after many a kind shake from the host, and just another drop of his sweeten'd, off they jogged, see-sawing from side to side on the critter, the old lady muttering her happiness, and the old man too full to find words to express himself.

"Sich another man as that Major," says she, "ain't nowhere—and sich a mixtur' as he *does* make, is temptin' to temperance lecturers. He is an amazin' nice man, and, if any thing, he sweetens the last drop better than the first. Good gracious! what a pleasin' creatur' he is!"

Ever and anon these enconiums on the Major and his mixture broke from the old lady, until of a sudden, on passing a small rivulet, a jolt of the mare's silenced them, and the old man rode on a short distance in perfect quietness. At length he broke out with—

"Old woman, you and that 'ere Major's conduct, to-day, war *rayther* unbecomin'—his *formalities* war too sweet to be mistook, and you ain't goin' *thar* agin in a hurry."

Silence, was the only answer.

"Oh, you're huffy, are you?" continued the old man. "Well, I guess you can stay so, till you give in," and on he jogged, in a silently jealous mood. On arriving at the farm, he called to a negro to lift the old woman off, but *Sam*, the nigger, stood gazing at him in silent astonishment.

"Lift her off, you Sam, do you hear?—and do it carefully, or some of her wrath'll bile out. In spite of the Major's sweetenin' she's mad as thunder."

"Why, de lor', massa, de ole 'oman aint dar," replied Sam, his eyes standing out of his countenance. "Jest turn round, massa, and satisfy you'self dat de ole 'oman clar gone an missin—*de lor'!*"

And sure enough, on a minute examination by the old man, she *was* "found missing." The Major was charged at once with abduction, instant measures were taken for pursuit, and a party despatched to scour the roads. On proceeding about two miles on the road to the Major's, the party were suddenly halted at the small rivulet, by finding the Missus with her head lying partly in the little stream, its waters laving her lips, and softly murmuring—"Not a drop more, Major, *unless it's sweeten'd!*"

NETTLE BOTTOM BALL;

OR, BETSY JONES' TUMBLE IN THE MUSH PAN.

"WELL, it *are* a fact, boys," said Jim Sikes, "that I promised to tell you how I cum to git out in these Platte diggins, and I speculate you mout as well have it at onst, kase its bin troublin' my conscience amazin' to keep it kiver'd up. The afarr raised jessy in Nettle Bottom, and old Tom Jones' *yell*, when he swar he'd 'chaw me up,' gives my meat a slight sprinklin' of ager whenever I think on it.

"You see, thar wur a small town called Equality, in Illin*ise*, that some speckelators started near Nettle Bottom, cos thar wur a spontaneos salt lick in the diggins, and no sooner did they git it agoin' and build some stores and groceries thar, than they wagon'd from Cincinnate and other up-stream villages, a pacel of fellers to attend the shops, that looked as nice, all'ays, as if they wur goin' to meetin' or on a courtin' frolic; and 'salt their picters,' they wur etarnally pokin' up their noses at us boys of the Bottom. Well, they got up a ball in the village, jest to interduce themselves to the gals round the neighborhood, and invited a few on us to make a contrary picter to themselves, and so shine us out of site by comparison. Arter that ball thur wan't any thin' talked on among the gals but what nice fellers the clerks in Equality wur, and how nice and slick they wore their *har*, and their shiny boots, and the way they stirrupp'd down their trowsers. You couldn't go to see one on 'em, that she wouldn't stick one of these fellers at you, and keep a talkin' how slick they looked. It got to be parfect pizen to hear of, or see the critters, and the boys got together at last to see what was to be done—the thing had grown parfectly alarmin'. At last a meetin' was agreed on, down to old Jake Bents'.

"On next Sunday night, instead of takin' the gals to meetin', whar they could see these fellers, we left 'em at home, and met at Jake's, and I am of the opinion thur was some congregated wrath thar—whew wan't they?

"'Oil and scissors!' says Mike Jelt, 'let's go down and lick the town, *rite strait!*'

"'No!' hollered Dick Butts, 'let's kitch these slick badgers comin' out of meetin', and tare the hide and feathers off on 'em!'

"'Why, darn 'em, what d'ye think, boys,' busted in old Jake, 'I swar if they ain't larnt our gals to wear *starn cushins;* only this mornin' I caught my darter Sally puttin' one on and tyin' it round her. She tho't I was asleep, but I seed her, and I made the jade *re-pudiate* it, and *no* mistake—*quicker!*'

"The boys took a drink on the occasion, and Equality town was slumberin', for a short spell, over a *con*-tiguous yearthquake. At last one of the boys proposed, before we attacked the town, that we should git up a ball in the Bottom, and jest out-shine the town chaps, all to death, afore we swallowed 'em. It was hard to gin in to this proposition, but the boys cum to it at last, and every feller started to put the afarr agoin'.

"I had been a long spell hankerin' arter old Tom Jones' darter, on the branch below the Bottom, and she *was* a critter good for weak eyes—maybe she hadn't a pair of her own—well, if they warn't a brace of movin' light-houses, I wouldn't say it—there was no calculatin' the extent or handsomeness of the family that gal could bring up around her, with a feller like me to look arter 'em. Talk about gracefulness, did you ever see a maple saplin' movin' with a south wind?—It warn't a crooked stick to compar' to her, but her old dad was *awful.* He could jest lick anythin' that said *boo*, in them diggins, out swar Satan, and was cross as a she *bar*, with cubs. He had a little hankerin' in favor of the fellers in town, too, fur they gin him presents of powder to hunt with, and he was precious fond of usin' his shootin' iron. I detarmin'd, anyhow, to ask his darter Betsy to be my partner at the Nettle Bottom Ball.

"Well, my sister Marth made me a bran new pair of buckskin trowsers to go in, and rile my pictur, ef she didn't put stirrups to 'em to keep 'em down. She said *straps* wur the fashion, and I should ware 'em. I jest felt with 'em on, as ef I had somethin' pressin' on me down—all my joints wur sot tight together, but Marth insisted, and I knew I could soon dance 'em off, so I gin in, and started off to the branch for Betsy Jones.

"When I arriv, the old fellar wur sittin' smokin' arter his supper, and the younger Jones' wur sittin' round the table, takin' theirs. A whappin' big pan of *mush* stood rite in the centre, and a large pan of milk beside it, with lots of corn bread and butter, and Betsy was helpin' the youngsters, while old Mrs. Jones sot by. admirin' the family collection. Old Tom took a hard star' at me, and I kind a shook, but the *straps* stood it, and I recovered myself, and gin him as good as he sent, but I wur near the door, and ready to break if he show'd fight.

"'What the h—ll are you doin' in *disgise*,' says the old man—he swore dreadfully—'are you comin' down here to steal?'

"I riled up at that. Says I, 'ef I wur comin' fur sich purpose, you'd be the last I'd hunt up to steal off on.'

"'You're right,' says he, 'I'd make a hole to light your innards, ef you did.' And the old savage chuckled. *I* meant because he had nothin' worth stealin', but his darter, but he tho't 'twas cos I was afear'd on him.

"Well, purty soon I gether'd up and told him what I cum down fur, and invited him to come up and take a drink, and see that all went on rite. Betsy was in an awful way fur fear he wouldn't consent. The old 'oman here spoke in favour of the move, and old Tom thought of the licker, and gin in to the measure. Off bounced Betsy up a ladder into the second story, and one of the small gals with her, to help put on the fix-ups. I sot down in a cheer, and fell a talkin' at the old 'oman. While we wur chattin' away as nice as relations, I could hear Betsy makin' things stand round above. The floor was only loose boards kivered over wide joice, and every step made 'em shake and rattle like a small hurricane. Old Tom smoked away and the young ones at the table would hold a spoonful of mush to thur mouths and look at my straps, and then look at each other and snigger, till at last the old man seed 'em.

"'Well, by gun flints,' says he, 'ef you ain't makin' a josey——'

"Jest at that moment, somethin' gin way above, and

may I die, ef Betsy, without any thin' on yearth on her but one of these *starn cushins*, didn't drop rite through the floor, and sot herself, *flat into the pan of mush!* I jest tho't fur a second, that heaven and yearth had kissed each other, and squeezed me between 'em. Betsy squealed like a 'scape pipe,—a spot of the mush had spattered on the old man's face, and burnt him, and he swore dreadful. I snatched up the pan of milk, and dashed it over Betsy to cool her off,—the old 'oman knocked me sprawlin' fur doing it, and away went my *straps*. The young ones let out a scream, as if the infarnal pit had broke loose, and I'd jest gin half of my hide to have bin out of the old man's reach. He did *reach* fur me, but I lent him one with my half-lows, on the smeller, that spread him, and maybe I didn't leave *sudden!* I didn't see the branch, but as I soused through it, I heerd Tom Jones swar he'd '*chaw me up*, ef an inch big of me was found in them diggins in the mornin'.

"I did'nt know fur a spell whar I was runnin', but hearing nuthin' behind me, I slacked up, and jest considered whether it was best to go home and git my traps strait, and leave, or go see the ball. Bein' as I was a manager, I tho't I'd go have a peep through the winder, to see ef it cum up to my expectations. While I was lookin' at the boys goin' it, one on 'em spied me, and they hauled me in, stood me afore the fire, to dry, and all hands got round, insistin' on knowin' what was the matter. I ups and tells all about it. I never heerd such laffin', hollerin', and screamin', in all my days.

"Jest then, my trowsers gin to feel the fire, and shrink up about an inch a minit, and the boys and gals kept it up so strong, laffin at my scrape, and the pickle

I wur in, that I gin to git riley, when all at onst I seed one of these slick critters, from town, rite in among' em, hollerin' wuss than the loudest.

" 'Old Jones said he'd chaw you up, did he?' says the town feller, '*well, he all'ays keeps his word.*'

"That minit I biled over. I grabbed his slick *har*, and may be I didn't gin him *scissors!* Jest as I was makin' him a *chawed specimen*, some feller holler'd out, —'don't let *old Jones* in with that ar *rifle!*' I didn't hear any more in that Bottom,—lightnin' could'nt a got near enough to singe my coat tail. I jumped through that winder as easy as a bar 'ud go through a cane brake; and cuss me if I could'nt hear the grit of old Jones' teeth, and smell his glazed powder, until I crossed old Massissippi."

A "CAT" STORY,

WHICH MUST NOT BE *CUR*-TAILED.

Ben Snaggletree seated himself in our society the other day, overburdened with a Mississippi yarn, which embraced one of his hair breadth 'scapes, and which he had resolved on relieving his memory of, by having it chronicled.

Ben was an old Mississip' *roarer*—none of your half and half, but just as native to the element, as if he had been born in a *broad horn*. He said he had been *fotched* up on the river's brink, and "knew a snappin' *turtle* from a *snag*, without larnin'."

"One night," says Ben, "about as dark as the face of Cain, and as unruly as if the elements had been untied, and let loose from their great Captain's command, I was on the old Mississippi; it was, in short, a night ugly enough to make any natural born Christian think of his prayers, and a few converted saints tremble—I walked out upon the steam boat 'guard' to cool off from the effects of considerable liquor doin's, participated in during the day, but had scacely reached the side of the boat, when she struck a snag, and made a lurch, throwing me about six feet into the *drink*. I was sufficiently cool, *stranger*, when I came to the surface, but I had nigh, in a short time, set the Mississippi a *bilin'*, my carcase grew so hot with wrath at observing the old boat wending her way up stream, unhurt, while I, solitary, unobserved, and alone, was floating on the old father of waters. I swam to the head of a small island, some distance below where we struck, and no sooner touched ground than I made an effort to stand erect. You may judge of my horror on discovering my landing place to be a Mississippi *mud-bar*, and about as firm as quicksand, into which I sunk about three feet in a moment.

"All was dark as a stack of black cats—no object visible save the lights of the receding boat—no sound smote upon the ear but the lessening blow of the 'scape pipe, and the plashing of the surrounding waters;—the first sounded like the farewell voice of hope, while the latter, in its plashing and purling, was like to the jabbering of evil spirits, exulting over an entrapped victim.

"I attempted to struggle, but that sunk me faster. I cried out, but fancied that, too, forced me deeper into my yielding grave; ere daylight dawned I felt sure of being *out of sight*, and the horrid thought of thus sinking into eternity through a *mud-gate*, made every hair stand 'on its own hook,' and forced my heart to patter against my ribs like a trip-hammer. I had been in many a scrape, but I considered this the nastiest, and made up my mind that the ball of yarn allotted to me was about being spun out—my cake was all *mud!* I promised old Mississippi, if permitted to escape this time, I would *lick* anythin' human that said a word agin her; but it was no use—she was sure of me now, and, like old 'bare bones' to an expiring African, she held on, and deeper, and deeper I sunk. In a short time I was forced to elevate my chin to keep out of my mouth an over-supply of the temperance liquid, which was flowing so coaxingly about my lips. My eyebrows were starting, my teeth set, and hope had wasted to a misty shadow, when something touched me like a floating solid; I instantly grasped it—it slid through my hands—*all but the tail*—which I clung to with a grip of *iron*.

"I soon discovered I had made captive a mammoth *catty*, huge enough to be the patriarch of his tribe, and a set of resolutions were quickly adopted in my mind, that he couldn't travel further without company. A desperate start and vigorous wiggle to escape was made by my friend, the *catty*, but there was six feet in length of *desperation* attached to his extremity, that could neither be coaxed or shook off. Soon succeeded another start, and out I came like a cork from a bottle. Off started the fish, like a comet, and after him I went, a *muddy spark* at the end of his tail. By a dexterous twist of his rudder, I succeeded in keeping him on the surface, and steered him to a solid landing, where I let him loose, and we shook ourselves, mutually pleased at parting company."

"That will do, Ben," said we, "all but the *tail*."

"Tail and all, or none!" said Ben, so here you have it. Ben swears he'll father it himself."

A SPIRITUAL SISTER.

HER ENCOUNTER WITH A DOUBTFUL SMITH.

"THERE goes Smith, the *Attorney*," said a man to his friend; as a tall figure, slightly stooped, hurried by them.

"I beg your pardon," answered the friend, "that is the Rev. Mr. Smith, a *preacher*, I have heard him in Tennessee."

"Well that's curious," replied the first, "for I'd swear *I* have heard him plead at the bar."

"Good morning Sol., how are you?" salutes another, as he hurries by a group of citizens.

"What did you call him?" inquired one of the party.

"Why, Sol. Smith, was the answer—*old* Sol., the *manager* of the theatre, to-be-sure; who did you suppose it was?—I thought you knew him—every body knows old *Sol!*"

"Well that is funny," answered the second, "for *I'll* swear he officiated as a *physician* on board our boat."

"Well who the d—l *is* he?"

This question was asked so frequently on board of a boat, recently, that those who didn't know became quite feverish, and those who did, kept dark to watch for a joke. Sol. had purchased a *new hat*—venerably broad in brim, of saintly and unostentatious height in crown, and it was easy to see that this new beaver was brewing him trouble. We feel almost inclined here to go into a disquisition upon hats, and the evils they have entailed, for who has not suffered, and been thrust out of the pale of good living, or cut in the street—or taken for a loafer, and asked by some dandy to hold his horse, or by some matron to carry home her market basket, and all because of a "shocking bad hat." An "old hat" is, in fact, dangerous—so is a new one of a peculiar shape—so was Sol.'s broad brimmer.

On board the steamer was a Mormon sister, on her way from down east to the holy city of Nauvoo, and many and anxious were her inquiries if any brother of the church was on board? None were able to inform her. At length the captain, at table, inquired:

"Shall I help you to a little of this roast beef, Mr. Smith?"

"Thank you, a small piece," was the reply.

"Smith," said the sister, "*Smith*, that's a member, jest as shure as shutin'; I'll get interduced tu him arter a spell, and I reckon he'll turn eout tu be a shure enough brother."

"Arter a spell" she did, through the kindness of the captain, get an introduction to him, and was previously informed by the commander, that Sol. was not only a shure enough Mormon, but an elder—in fact a *Smith!* Sol., as usual, was courteous and affable as when introduced to little Vic., at the court of St. James, and the *sister* was "tickled all tu death" at the idea of falling in with so pleasant an elder. She was a little ancient, but buxom, and Sol. felt flattered by her singling him out for an acquaintance.

"I'd a know'd in a minit that you was a member of the church by your countenance and your *hat*, Brother Smith, you *do* look so saintly."

"Yes, Ma'm," answered he, "most people take me for a member."

"I was a thinkin' if you hadn't chosen a—he-he-he—a sister, why—"—*Page 69.*

"There's ony one thing, Brother Smith, which appears rayther queer about *our* church," said she, looking modestly at Sol., and biting the corner of her handkerchief, "and that's the 'new system' they have interduced."

"Why, yes,—y-e-s," said Sol., at fault, "'new systems' do trouble the church a good deal."

"Law, Brother Smith, do *you* think the 'speritual system' a trouble?"

"Well, no, not exactly, if it's a good spiritual teaching," answered he, "it's only the false doctrines that are evil."

"Well, that's jest what Elder Adams sed down in eour parts, and he ses that it was speritually revealed tu the Prophet Joseph, your brother, and I was jest a thinkin'," and here she spread her handkerchief over her face, and twisted her head to one side,—"I was a thinkin' if *you* hadn't chosen a—he-he-he!—a *sister*, why,"——

"We're at a landing, Ma'm, excuse me for a moment," and off shot Sol. to his state room, where he seized a pair of well worn saddle-bags, and his *old hat*, which he had thus far carried with him, intending to have it brushed up, and started for the gang-way plank. The captain met him in his haste, and inquired where he was going?

"Why, captain," says Sol., "I like your boat vastly, and you know I like you, but there might be a 'blow up' if I stayed on board much longer."

"Explain," says the captain.

"Why, the fact is," said Sol., "that lady you introduced me to has taken me for the *Mormon* Smith; now, I'm a good many Smith's when my family and titles are all collected, but I aint *that* Smith! Just tell her so for me, and give her my 'old hat'—it's the best I can do for her." We needn't add that Brother Smith was straightway among the missing!

HOSS ALLEN'S APOLOGY;

OR, THE CANDIDATE'S NIGHT IN A MUSQUITO SWAMP!

"WELL, old fellow, you're a *hoss!*" is a western expression, which has grown into a truism as regards Judge Allen, and a finer specimen of a western judge, to use his constituents' language, "aint no whar," for, besides being a sound jurist, he is a great wag, and the best practical joker within the circuit of six states. Among the wolf-scalp hunters of the western border of Missouri, Judge, or, as they more familiarly style him, *Hoss* Allen is all *powerful* popular, and the "bar" hunters of the southern section equally admire his free and easy manners—they consider him one of the people—none of your stuck-up imported chaps from the dandy states, but a real genuine westerner—in short, a *hoss!* Some of the Judge's admirers prevailed upon him, recently, to stand a canvass for the gubernatorial chair, in which he had Judge Edwards for an antagonist, and many are the rich jokes told of their political encounters. A marked difference characterizes the two men, and more striking opposites in disposition and demeanor would be hard to find, Edwards being slow, dignified, and methodical, while *Hoss* tosses dignity to the winds, and comes right down to a free and easy familiarity with the "boys." Hoss Allen counted strong on the border counties, while his antagonist built his hopes on the centre.

Allen and Edwards had travelled together for a number of days, explaining their separate views upon state government, at each regular place of appointment, and were now nearing the southern part of the state, a section where *Hoss* had filled the judgeship with great unction. Here he resolved to spring a joke upon his antagonist, which would set the south laughing at him, and most effectually insure his defeat among the *bar* hunters. He had been maturing a plan, as they journeyed together, and now having stopped for the night about one day's journey from the town of Benton, one of their places of appointment, and the head quarters of the most influential men of the *bar* section, Hoss proceeded to put his trick in progress of execution. He held a secret conference, at the stable, with the boy who took his horse, and offered him a dollar to take a message that night to Tom Walters, at the forks leading to Benton. The boy agreed, and Hoss penciled a note describing his antagonist, who was unknown in the south of the state, coupled with an earnest request, that he "would keep a look out for Judge Eddards, and by all means be careful not to let him get into that cussed *cedar swamp!*" His express was faithful, and in due time Tom received the missive. In the meantime, the victim, Edwards, in a sweet state of confidence, was unbending his dignity at hearing Hoss relate to their host his amusing yarns about the early settlers. Having talked all the household into a merry mood, he proposed turning in for the night, but first offered his service to unlace the girls' corsets, and in an underbreath asked the old woman to *elope* with him in the morning—Edwards blushed at this, the girls tittered, and the host and his wife said, he was a "raal *hoss!*" —Allen acknowledged he was a leetle inclined that way, and as he had had his *feed*, he now wanted his *straw*.

In the morning Hoss Allen became "dreadful poorly," and it was with great difficulty he could be prevailed upon to get up. All were sympathising with his affliction, and the matron of the house boiled him some hot "sass-tea," which, the old man said, relieved him mightily. Judge Edwards assured Hoss, that it would be necessary for him to lay up for a day or two, and the afflicted candidate signified the same, himself. Before they parted Hoss requested Edwards, as he had the whole field to himself, not to be too *hard* upon him. His antagonist promised to spare him, but chuckled all the while at having a clear field in Allen's most popular district. Shaking the old *Hoss* by the hand, as they were about to separate, he remarked—"we will meet at Benton, I hope, in different trim, Friend Allen." They *did* meet in different *trim*, but Edwards little dreamed the particular kind of trim *he* would appear in. As soon as Judge Edwards was fairly started, it was surprising the rapid change which took place in his antagonist —Hoss' eye lit up, a broad grin spread over his features, and pulling off the handkerchief, which was tied around his head, he twirled it above him like a flag, then stuffed it in his pocket, remarking coolly, at the same time,— "well, that thar swamp, jest at this season, is *awful!*" His express reported himself after his night ride, assured Allen that all was O. K., and received his dollar for delivering the message, upon receiving which intelligence, Allen seated himself quietly and comfortably at his coffee, and imbibed it with a relish that drove the idea of sickness into a hopeless decline.

Judge Edwards rapidly progressed on his way, highly gratified at having his opponent off in this part of the field, and as he, in this happy mood, journeyed onwards he set his brain to work conning a most powerful speech, one that would knock the sand from under Hoss, and leave him in a state of sprawling defeat. He resolved to sweep the south, from that point, like a prairie fire. About noon, or perhaps an hour after, he arrived at Tom Walters' for dinner, and while it was preparing, inquired how far he was from Benton?

"I've an idea," said Tom, "you're well onto nine miles frum thar—jest an easy arternoon ride."

This was highly satisfactory to the Judge, and perceiving that the provender preparing was of a like pleasing character, he spread himself back upon a hickory bottomed chair with a kind of easy dignity, at once comfortable to himself, and edifying to his host.

"Stranger," inquired Tom, "did you *scare* up anythin' like the two candidates, Jedge Eddards and old Hoss Allen, on your way down *yeur?*"

"I did see something of them, my friend," answered the Judge, and then, as if making up his mind to surprise Tom, and give him a striking example of democratic condescension, he inquired, "would you know either of the gentlemen, if they stood before you?"

"Why, as to old Hoss," said Tom, "I don't know anybody else, but this new Jedge I ain't never seed, and ef he is the slicked up finefied sort on a character they pictur' him, I don't *want* to see him—Its my opinion, these squirtish kind a fellars ain't perticular hard baked, and they allers goes in fur *a*ristocracy notions."

The Judge had no idea that Tom was smoking him, and he congratulated himself that an opportunity here presented itself, where he could remove a wrong impression personally; so, loftily viewing this southern constituent, be remarked:

"You have heard a calumny, my friend, for *Judge* Edwards now sits before you, and you can see whether his appearance denotes such a person as you describe."

"No!" shouted Tom, with mock surprise, "you aint comin' a hoax over a fellar?—you raally are the sure enough Jedge?"

"I am really the Judge, my friend," responded his honor, highly elevated with Tom's astonishment.

"Then gin us your paw," shouted Tom, "you're jest the lookin' fellar kin sweep these yeur diggins like a catamount! What in the yearth did you do with old Hoss on the road? I heerd he was a comin' along with you. He aint gin out, has he?"

The Judge replied, with a smile which expressed disparagement of Hoss Allen's powers of endurance, that he was forced to lie up on the route, from fatigue. Dinner being announced as ready the Judge and Tom seated themselves, and the latter highly expanded his guest's prospects in the district, assuring him that he could lick Hoss "powerful easy, ef he wasn't broken winded." The meal being ended, the Judge demanded his horse, and inquired of his host the direct road to Benton, which Tom thus mapped out:—

"Arter you pass the big walnut, about two miles from yeur, keep *it* a mile on your left, and take the right trail fur about six hundred yards, when you'll cum to the 'saplin acre,' thar you keep to the right agin, and when that trail fotches you up, why right *over from thar* lies Benton."

This was a very clear direction to one who had never

before travelled the road, but the Judge, trusting to luck, said, "he thought he would be able to get there without much difficulty," and started off, leaving his late entertainer gazing after him.

"Well, I allow you *will*, Jedge," chuckled Tom,—"You'll git inter that *swamp*, jest as sure as shootin', and you'll hev the biggest and hungryest audience of mosquitors, ever a candidate preached law or larnin' to!" To secure his finding the swamp road, he had stationed his boy *Jim* near the turn off, to make the matter sure.

In the course of a couple of hours along came Hoss Allen, who, as soon as Tom took hold of his bridle, winked his eye at him while he inquired:—

"Did Jedge Eddards come along, Tom?"

"Well, he *did*, Hoss, oncommon extensive in his political feelins'."

"And you didn't let the Jedge stray away from the swamp road?" inquired Hoss.

"Well, I predicate I didn't, fur by this time he's travellin' into the diggins most amazin' innocently," and then the pair enjoyed a regular guffaw!

"He's safe as a skin'd *bar*, then, Tom, and I'll spread his hide afore the Benton boys to-morrow—jest let them into the joke, and I allow, after that, his dandified *a*ristocracy speeches won't have much effect in this section.

"Go it, Jedge," shouted Tom, "ef I ain't thar to hear it, it'll be 'cause the breath'll leave me afore then—gin him goss without sweeten'—rumple his har, but don't spile the varmint!"

After Hoss had stayed his stomach with a cold bite, he bade Tom good-day, and started for Benton, highly tickled with the success of his trick. As he neared the "saplin acre," he met *Jim*, who exhibited a full spread of his ivories, when Hoss inquired which road he had directed the gentleman before him?

"He gone into de swamp road, massa, but what de debil he want dar, 'cept he arter coon skins, dis niggah doesn't hab no idear, whatsomedeber."

Allen passed on, assured that all was right, and as his horse leisurely ambled forward, he broke into singing a verse of a western ditty, which says:—

"Thar aint throughout this western nation,
Another like old Hickory
He was born jest fur his siteation—
A bold leader of the free."

As night spread her curtain over this wild district, Hoss neared Benton, and as his nag jogged up the principal street, he broke out into a louder strain, repeating the above verse, on hearing which, the "boys," who were expecting him and Edwards, turned out, and old Hoss was received with a cheer.

"Hello, Jedge!—How are you, Old Hoss?—Give us your paw, Governor!—Here at last, Squire!"—and sundry such expressions of familiar welcome was showered on Allen, by the crowd "Come in, and git a drink, old fellar," shouted one of the crowd, and forthwith all hands pushed for the hotel bar room, where sweetened corn juice was pushed about with vast liberality—at the *candidate's* expense, of course.

"Whar did you leave the new fellar, Jedge Eddards?" was the general inquiry.

"Why, boys, I stopped to rest on the road, and he slid off to git ahead of me—I heered on him at the forks, and expected he was here. It's my opinion, boys, he's seen a *bar* on the road, and bein' too delicate to make the varmint clar the path, he's taken a long circuit round him!"

This raised a laugh among the crowd, and it was followed up by general inquiries as to what Edwards looked like, but to these Hoss shook his head, remarking, as he raised his hands expressive of how they would be astonished—"jest wait tell you see him yourselves, boys, and then you'll be satisfied."

Let us return to Judge Edwards, who had easily found his way past the "sapling acre," and by the aid of Jim's direction progressed into the swamp road, as easy as if it were his destination. Having travelled, as he thought, about ten miles, he began to look out for Benton, and every now and then uttered an expression of surprise, that they had located the town in such a swampy country—every rod he progressed became more and more obscure, the brush more thick and wild in growth, and the ground more moist and yielding. Night, too, that season for the rendezvous of underbrush and tangle-wood horrors, was fast gathering its forces in the depths of the forest, and beneath the shadows of the thick bushes, shrouding, as with a dark mist, each object on the earth's surface, creeping up the trunks of the old trees, and noiselessly stealing away the light in which they had proudly spread their green foliage, while in lieu of their showy garb he clad them in a temporary mourning. The song of the birds became hushed, while the cry of the startled *wolf* was borne upon the breeze to the ear of the affrighted traveller, interrupted occasionally by the sharp *m-e-o-w!* of the wild-cat, making together a vocal concert [illegible] unharmonious to the ear of the bewildered candidate. To sum up these horrors a myriad of *mosquitoes*, as musical as hunger and vigorous constitutions could make them, hummed and fi-z-z-zed around him, darting in their stings and darting away from his annoyed blows, with a pertinacity and perseverance only known to the Missouri tribe of insects.

Poor Edwards!—he was fairly in for it—into a swamp at that!—Night was fast making all roads alike obscure, and with amazing rapidity covering our traveller in a mantle of uncertainty. The possibility of his escape that night first became improbable, and then impossible. He hallooed at the highest pitch of his voice, but the wolf was the only live varmint that answered his cry, and a strange fear began to creep over his heart. He remembered well reading accounts of where hungry droves of these animals had eaten the horse from under the saddle, the rider upon it, bones, hide, *har* and all, leaving scarce a vestige of the victims to mark the deed, and his hair grew uneasy on his cranium at the bare thought of such an unpolitical termination to his canvass. At this particular moment a *yell*, as of a thousand devils in his immediate neighbourhood, set his heart knocking against his ribs in a fearful manner. When he partially recovered from the shock he tied his horse to one tree and quickly mounted another—whispering the hope to his heart, at the same time, that a meal on his horse would satisfy the gathering crowd of varmints, who were shouting their death song below him. Having seated himself astride a limb, the mosquitoes had a fair chance at him, and they put the Judge through as active an exercise as ever was inflicted on a recruit—there was this difference, however, between him and a recruit, *they* are generally *raw* at the commencement of a drill, but poor Edwards was most *raw* at the end of his lesson. Every new yell of the swamp pre-emptioners, made him climb a limb higher, and each progression upwards appeared to introduce him to a fresh and hungrier company of mosquitoes—the trees in the swamp were like the dwellings in Paris, their *highest* tenants were the most needy. Day at length broke, and our harassed candidate, almost exhausted, clambered from his exalted position. His frightened but unscathed steed uttered a neigh of welcome as he bestrode him, and giving loose to the rein he committed his escape to the animal's sagacity, while he aided his efforts by a devout supplication. Accident favored the horse's footsteps, for striking the trail leading to the road he started off into a trot, and soon broke his rider's spell of terror, by turning into the main avenue leading to Benton. Edwards slowly passed his pimpled hand over his worse pimpled face, sadly remarking:—

"Last night's '*bills*' all passed, for I bear their stinging *signatures* all over my countenance."

When ten o'clock came, on the day following Judge Allen's arrival at Benton, the town swarmed with the southern constituency of Missouri, and as soon as the tavern bell, which had been put in requisition to announce the candidate's readiness, had ceased its clamor, Hoss mounted the balcony of the hotel, and rolling up his sleeves "spread himself" for an unusually brilliant effort.

"Boys!" shouted he, "I want your attention to matters of vital import—of oncommon moment, and replete with a nation's wel*far*." [Here looking down into the crowd at Sam Wilson, who was talking as loud as he could bellow, about an imported heifer he had just bought, Hoss called his attention:] "Sam," said he, "you'd better bring that heifer of your'n up here to address the meetin', and I'll wait till the animal gits through!" This raised a laugh on Sam, and Hoss proceeded. After dilating at some length on the *imported* candidate who was his antagonist, he "*let himself out*," on some of the measures he advocated, and particularly dwelt on the fact that he went in for creating a license law on hunting varmints!

"Would you have the least mite of an idea, boys," said Hoss, "that this creatur' of a faction wants to have every man's rifle stamped with the state arms, and then made pay a license to the state before he can git a bonus for wolf scalps." [At this moment a shrill voice interrupted him again—a girl belonging to the hotel was shouting to a couple of youngsters, who had been despatched to the barn for eggs, to "quit *suckin'* them thar eggs or the candidates would stand a mighty small chance fur thur dinner.] "Jest tell that gall," said Hoss, "to suck my share and stop her screamin'." He again continued: "I want to know what in yearth this Massissippi country's comin' too, when sich fellars finds favor with the people—what do you think of him boys?"

"Why, *cuss his pictur!*" was the general response from the *bar* hunters.

While Hoss was thus arousing public indignation against his antagonist, a stranger entered the crowd, and after listening a moment to the speaker's imaginary flights he interrupted him by shouting:—

"I deny your assertions, Judge Allen!"

This was a bomb shell, and the crowd cleared a space round the stranger, in expectation of a fight; but

Allen after surveying the stranger, in whom he recognised his antagonist Edwards, coolly inquired why *he* disputed it?

"What, *me!*" shouted Edwards, "who can better declare your assertions false than the man you are misrepresenting—you know very well that *I* am that Judge Edwards!"

Hoss Allen turned calmly round to the crowd and said:—"Boys, you know I never git angry at a man insane or in liquor, and as I don't know this fellar, and never seed him afore in my life, its the best proof that he aint Jedge Eddards, so you'll oblige me by taking him off the ground and keeping him from disturbing the meeting."

Expostulation was useless—without any ceremony he was carried into the hotel, boiling with indignation. There, however, he had to stay, at a convenient distance to hear that Allen was giving him "*particular jesse.*"

After the meeting adjourned three cheers were given for Hoss Allen, and all parties gathered into the bar to take a little *fluid*, and discuss the speech. Edwards having now been relieved from durance, started for Hoss;—burning inside with choler and smarting exteriorly from mosquito-bites,—he looked *bitter*.

"Do you say you don't know me, Judge Allen?" inquired he.

Hoss looked steadily at him, then coolly taking out his spectacles, he wiped the glasses, adjusted them upon his nose, and surveyed the questioner from head to foot, he then remarked:

"Thar is somethin' about your voice, and the clothes you ware, that I ought to know—Jedge Eddards wore a coat and kerseys exactly like your'n, but I'll swar he had a better lookin' face than you carry when we parted yesterday mornin'. If you are him you're been the wust used candidate I've seed in an age."

"Yes," responded Edwards, "thanks to that d—n nigger that sent me into the swamp. I tell you sir that I have passed a night to which the infernal regions are a scant pattern, and between mosquitoes, wolves, and wild-cats I should not be surprised if my hair had turned grey."

"I begin to *re*-cognise you, now, Jedge," said Hoss, in a sympathetic tone, "and no wonder I didn't know you at first sight—your head is swelled as big as a *pumkin!* I'll do the clean thing, Jedge," said Hoss, starting for the balcony, I'll apologise afore the boys, publicly, for not knowin' you."

"No, no!" shouted Edwards, who knew his apology would only place his night's adventure in a more ridiculous light, "I don't demand any apology." But he was too late, Hoss had already called the attention of the crowd.

"Boys," said he, "as an honourable man who finds himself in the wrong, I am bound to apologise, publicly, to my friend Jedge Eddards,—the Jedge is a leetle changed in appearance since we wur last together, and I did not *re*-cognise him; I, tharfore, ask his pardon fur orderin' him off the ground."

"I grant it!" shouted Edwards, glad here to wind up the apology, then turning round he added, "come boys, let us drink good friends."

"Wait a minit, boys," said Hoss, "the Jedge and I havin' smoothed that little marter over, I jest want to tell you why I didn't know him at fust sight. You all know that the mosquitoes in cedar swamp are an *oreful* hungry breed, and when they git a passenger they present him with numerous 'relief bills;' well I had gained considerable popularity in that swamp, by presentin' their condition before the legislatur' and askin' for reliet for the distressed inhabitants,—the Jedge, to head me down thar, passed all last night on a limb of one of the trees makin' stump speeches to the varmints, and you can see by his countenance that expectin' to be elected he has accepted all their *mosquito bills!*"

One tremendous shout rent the air, followed by bursts of laughter, from which Edwards retreated into the hotel. We have but to add that Hoss carried the *Bar* counties "as easy as rolling off a log!" His antagonist in vain tried to stem the tide of fun,—when he essayed to speak a *m-e-o-w* of a wild-cat or the *hum* of a mosquito imitated by some of his audience would be sure to set the rest *sniggering*, and spoil his effort.

NATURAL ACTING!

DAN MARBLE'S FIRST APPEARANCE AT GRAND RIVER, MICHIGAN.

SEVERAL years since our friend Dan Marble, the celebrated representative of Yankee characters, was performing an engagement at Detroit, and was persuaded by some friends to take a trip to Chicago, and give them a taste of his quality in the lake city. Dan consented, and on board of the good steamer Constitution, commanded by a skilful captain, under the care of Doty, one of the best lake engineers, and piloted by

Gus. McKinstry, they set out in the fall of the year for their northern destination. All went "merry as a marriage bell;" they had a successful trip up,—Dan. had a successful engagement—and back they started for Detroit. But now the elements became rebellious; whether rude Boreas resolved to keep this favorite son of Momus up there in his northern home, we know not, but when the vessel that bore his fortunes—his own comical self—had nearly reached the head of the lake, against a head wind that would almost tear off a shirt collar, they run out of woŏd, and was forced to scud back to Milwaukee a "leetle dust faster than they wanted tu." They loaded up with the fuel again, and shutting their teeth with determination, they fastened tight the safety valve, and tried it again right in the teeth of the hurricane. After puffing, and blowing, and wheezing, and coughing, the old boat had to give in, and hunt a harbor. Fate drove them into Grand River—we say, Fate did it, in order, as we think, to keep up the character of a *grand* stream by opening a dramatic temple on its banks, with an exhibition of the budding greatness of a genius. Fate, you know, has the ordering of such things.

The noble steamer came to anchor in the quiet river, between its towering sand banks, and old "blow hard" tossed the lake wave on the outside, top-mast high, with glee, at having penned Dan. Down came an inhabitant of the town of Grand River, who had seen Dan. perform at Buffalo, and recognising him, up he posted to spread the news. In the meantime, those on board were wondering how they should pass the weary hours, if the fierce wind continued its fury. Presently, down comes another resident to the boat, a small *cat-skin cap* on his head, a Canada-mixed coat on, and dressed in *deer-skin breeches.*

"Whar is *he*?—which is *him*?—consarn his comic pictur, show him out—ha-ha-ha!"

"Who are you lookin' after, Mister?" inquired the pilot.

"Why Dan—corn twist him—Dan Marble, to be sure."

"Well, here I am, old fellar," answered the pilot, "take a look at me!" The pilot weighed about two hundred and twenty-two pounds, and had on an old sou-wester tarpaulin. Back stepped the inhabitant of Grand River, as if to get a good look, and take in all his dimensions at one stare. Gus, the pilot, made a wry face at his cat-skin observer, and out he burst:

"Ha-ha-ha!—ho-ho-ho!—he-he-he!—cuss me ef you ain't jest as I heerd on you—we've got you, have we? ha-ha-ha!—stop till I go and get the fellars, and by grist mills you'll have to gin us a playin'!" and forthwith off started the cat-skin cap and deer-skin breeches, their owner pausing every hundred yards to ejaculate—

"Ha-ha!—we've got him!"

In a short time he returned, sure enough, and half the town with him. A number of the business men of the place waited upon Dan, proper, and requested that he would amuse them, and pass away his own time, by relating some of his Yankee stories, singing songs, &c., tendering him, at the same time, the second story of a storehouse for his theatre. Dan consented, and all hands on board entering into the spirit of the thing, they soon constructed a temporary stage, with a sail for a back scene and the American flag for a curtain.

Night came, and with its shadows came the inhabitants of the town of Grand River—the owner of the *cat-skin cap* and his party, among the number.

In order to make his performance varied, Dan made arrangements to produce the *skunk scene*, from the "Water Witch;" and drilled Doty, the engineer, Gus, the pilot, the clerk of the boat, and the mate, to perform the English sailors in the scene. It will be remembered by those who have witnessed it, that they catch the Yankee just as he has killed a skunk, and are about to press him as a sailor; he persuades them to see a specimen of his shooting—they stick up the dead animal as a mark, and while he gets their attention upon the object in one direction, he retreats in the other, showing off in his exit a specimen of "tall walking." After considerable drilling his assistants were pronounced perfect; but the pilot swore that, to play an English sailor, he must get *disguised*, so accordingly he primed with a double quantity of grog. His associates, jealous of his natural acting, say he had to get drunk before he could look at the audience. Up went the curtain, and on went Dan; of course the audience were amused—they couldn't help it; but cat-skin looked in vain for *his* Dan. At length the skunk scene opened, and on came the pilot at the head of his party. The deer-skin breeches could hardly hold their owner; he ha-ha'd and ho-ho'd as if he would go into fits. Gus clapped his eye upon him, and screwed up his face into as many lines as a map, which finished the effect with cat-skin—he rolled off his seat, almost convulsed. Now commenced the scene with Yankee Dan, and when he told Gus to stoop down and watch his shot, it was with considerable difficulty that the pilot balanced himself in any such position. While they were stooping, off started Dan in their rear, and, to keep up the scene, off they started in pursuit; Dan, according to plot, hid behind the R. H. wing, front—his pursuers should here pass him and cross the stage, allowing him, by a Yankee trick, to escape; but that portion of the plot Gus, the pilot, had forgotten; he, therefore, came to a dead halt and looked round for Dan; there he was, and out shouted Gus: "Come out, old fellar—I see you!"

Dan shook his head and signed for them to go on.

"No you don't," says the pilot; "we caught you fair, and I'm be d—d if you shan't *treat!*"

The effect was irresistible; Dan had to give in, and the curtain dropped before a delighted audience—a collapsed pair of deer-skin breeches, and upon the first night of the drama in Grand River. The owner of the cat-skin cap and deer-skin breeches maintains, to this day, that the pilot *was* Dan Marble.

"Them other fellars," says he, "done pooty well, but any 'coon, with half an eye, could see that that *fat* fellar did the *naturalest acting!*

A CANAL ADVENTURE.

"Oh hapless our fate was, each one and all,
For we were wreck-*ed* on the Erie Canal,"
Old Ballad.

ON an evening in the month of July, 1836, I embarked at Lockport, in company with some fourteen passengers, on board an Erie Canal packet, destined for Rochester. It will be remembered that this was during the great migrating period in the United States, when all nations and pursuits had representatives on our principal travelling routes. Our party was no sooner aboard than the "bold captain" gave the word, the horses were got "under weigh," the *feathers* set, and all hands called to pick out their *shelf*—a six foot-by-one convenience, suspended by cords—upon which they stowed away passengers for the night. Babel never heard a greater confusion of tongues than this call set wagging. But above them all was heard the silver tone of a travelling exquisite, piping out—

"I-aw am first, cap'en, really,—I claim pwior choice, I do, dem if I don't."

Happening to be first on the register, it was accorded, and the captain suggested a locker berth, as the most comfortable.

"No! no!—dem,—beg you-a pawden, cap'en," shouted the exquisite, "some gwos, fat individual, might get on the-a upa shelf and bweak down,—I should be mangled howibly."

"Be jabers, I'd like to hev the squazin of him, mesilf," said a burly Irishman.

"They'd better spill a leettle smellin' stuff on the pesky animal, or he'll spile before mornin'," chimed in a Yankee.

After sundry remarks, at the exquisite's expense, and considerable confusion, all were duly ticketed for the night, and commenced piling themselves away like pledges in a pawnbroker's shop. Jonathan and the Irishman carelessly spread themselves upon a couple of long cane-bottomed settees, which occupied the centre of the cabin, and, in a very brief space of time, the company hushed into silence, save an occasional short blessing bestowed upon the *short* berths. When all appeared to have dropped into forgetfulness, the head of a way-passenger was thrust into the cabin entrance, with the inquiry—

"Is there any *berths* here?"

"Sure, this is the *gintlemen's* cabin," answered the Irishman.

"Well, I want to know if there's any *berths* here?" reiterated the inquirer.

"Divil a chance for wan here," was the response; "don't I tell ye this is the *gintlemen's* cabin?"

This conversation partially aroused the sleepers, who inquired of the Emeralder what was the row?

"Some botherin' docthur," was the sleepily muttered reply.

All soon again relapsed into quiet;—snore began to answer snore, in "high and boastful *blowing*," and I turned my back to the lamp for the purpose of making a somnolent effort, individually. After tossing and turning for some time, I found that the plentiful supper taken at Lockport had entered a veto against sleep for me, and every effort failed to accomplish more than a drowsy lethargy, which still left the senses partially awake. A strange bumping noise aided to keep me in this state, and I was labouring to assign a cause for the sound, when a voice distinctly cried out—

"It's no use a pumpin', captin', and I *won't!* She may sink and be *dern'd!*"

The concluding part of this remark started my senses into activity, and, after an effort, I turned round on my foot-wide couch, and took a survey of my "sleeping partners," to observe how the voice had affected them; but not a muscle moved—all were chorussing beautifully the lays of dream-land. The certainty of our "sinking and be dern'd," was soon apparent, for the light of the lamp, suspended from the ceiling of the cabin, soon began to be reflected from the floor—the waters were quietly stealing upon the unconscious sleepers. My first impulse was to sound the alarm, but, fortunately, possessing a "top shelf," and conscious that we could sink but a few feet, I held my peace until the water should increase its depth, being sure of fun when I gave the signal.

A pair of boots now commenced a very fair *forward-two* to a boot-jack which was busily engaged in executing a *chassez* before a nodding hat,—stockings were wriggling about, as if pleased with the fun, and, in a few minutes more, all was a scene of life among the sleepers' "unconsidered trifles" of wardrobe carelessly cast upon the floor. The water having reached within a few inches of the slumbering pair upon the cane-bottomed settees, I sounded the alarm, by shouting—"Murder! boat's sinking! hurrah! help!" Off tumbled the Irishman and Yankee—splash—dash—flounder and exclamation!

"Holy Virgin! what's this?" inquired Pat.

"Cre-*a*-tion and the deluge!" shouted Jonathan

"Good gwacious!" piped in the dandy.

Down hopped the tenants of the shelves, like bodies in a family vault at the general rising—up again they hopped, light as *spirits* and twice as natural, the instant their pedal extremities touched the *water*.

"Take it *cool*, gentlemen," shouted a westerner, from a top berth, "these are the *canal extras*."

A lady, at this moment, parted the curtains of their cabin—the Emeralder, with true gallantry, seized her in his arms, with a shout of "Riscue the ladies!" and bore her out on deck. Jonathan, not to be outdone by a foreigner, stood ready for the second, but her weight (only two hundred pounds) put a stumper on his gallantry. Yankee ingenuity, however, overcame the difficulty,—by making a bridge of the cane settees, the ladies were safely conducted from their watery quarters.

It was a funny scene on deck, that night, and little ceremony was observed in making a toilet. None, however, seemed to take the matter seriously but the dandy—he had lost all his beautifying essentials, in the confusion, and was almost frightened to death at his hair-breadth 'scape. Jonathan was offering him some crumbs of comfort, to induce him to make a purchase for his future safety.

"I'll tell you what, Mister," says Jonathan, "jest buy one of my everlastin'-no-drownin'-dry-and-water-tight-life-presarvers, and when you git it *fixed right*, it'll keep you so dry you'll have to sprinkle yourself to *stick together*.

THE STANDING CANDIDATE.

HIS EXCUSE FOR BEING A BACHELOR.

At Buffalo Head, Nianga county, state of Missouri, during the canvass of 1844, there was held an extensive political *Barbecue*, and the several candidates for congress, legislature, county offices, &c., were all congregated at this southern point for the purpose of making an *immense* demonstration. Hards, softs, whigs and

Tylerites were represented, and to hear their several expositions of state and general policy, a vast gathering of the Missouri sovereigns had also assembled. While the impatient candidates were awaiting the signal to mount the "stump," an odd-looking old man made his appearance at the brow of a small hill bounding the place of meeting.

"Hurrah for old *Sugar!*" shouted an hundred voices, while on, steadily, progressed the object of the cheer.

Sugar, as he was familiarly styled, was an old man, apparently about fifty years of age, and was clad in a coarse suit of brown linsey-woolsey. His pants were patched at each knee, and around the ankles they had worn off into picturesque points—his coat was not of the modern close-fitting cut, but hung in loose and easy folds upon his broad shoulders, while the total absence of buttons upon this garment, exhibited the owner's contempt for the storm and the tempest. A coarse shirt, tied at the neck with a piece of twine, completed his body covering. His head was ornamented with an old woollen cap, of divers colors, below which beamed a broad, humorous countenance, flanked by a pair of short, funny little grey whiskers. A few wrinkles marked his brow, but time could not count them as sure chronicles of his progress, for *Sugar's* hearty, sonorous laugh oft drove them from their hiding place. Across his shoulder was thrown a sack, in each end of which he was bearing to the scene of political action, a keg of *bran new whiskey*, of his own manufacture, and he strode forward on his moccason covered feet, encumbered as he was, with all the agility of youth. *Sugar* had long been the *standing candidate* of Nianga county, for the legislature, and

OLD SUGAR: THE STANDING CANDIDATE.—*Page* 92.

founded his claim to the office upon the fact of his being the first "squatter" in that county—his having killed the first *bar* there, ever killed by a white man, and, to place his right beyond cavil, he had *'stilled* the first keg of whiskey! These were strong claims, which urged in his comic rhyming manner would have swept the "diggins," but *Sugar*, when the canvass opened, always yielded his claim to some liberal purchaser of his *fluid*, and duly announced himself a candidate for the *next* term.

"Here you air, old fellar!" shouted an acquaintance, "allays on hand 'bout 'lection."

"Well, Nat.," said *Sugar*, "you've jest told the truth as easy as ef you'd taken sum of my mixtur—

'Whar politicians congregate,
I'm allays thar, at any rate!'"

"Set him up!—set the old fellar up somewhar, and let us take a univarsal liquor!" was the general shout.

"Hold on, boys,—keep cool and shady," said old *Sugar*, "whar's the candidates?—none of your splurgin round till I git an appropriation fur the sperits. Send em along and we'll negotiate fur the *fluid*, arter which I shall gin 'em my instructions, and they may then *per*-cede to

'Talk away like all cre-*a*-tion,
What they knows about the nation.'"

The candidates were accordingly summoned up to pay for *Sugar's* portable grocery, and to please the crowd and gain the good opinion of the owner, they made up a purse and gathered round him. *Sugar* had placed his two kegs upon a broad stump and seated himself astride of them, with a small tin cup in his hand

and a paper containing brown sugar lying before him—each of his kegs was furnished with a *spiggot*, and as soon as the money for the whole contents was paid in, *Sugar* commenced addressing the crowd as follows:

"Boys, fellars, and candidates," said he, "I, *Sugar*, am the furst white man ever seed in these yeur diggins—I killed the furst *bar* ever a white skinned in this county, and I kalkilate I hev hurt the feelings of his relations sum sence, as the *bar-skin* linin' of my cabin will testify;—'sides that, I'm the furst manufacturer of whiskey in the range of this district, and powerful mixtur' it is, too, as the hull bilin' of fellars in this crowd will declar';—more'n that, I'm a candidate for the legislatur', and intend to gin up my claim, *this* term, to the fellar who kin talk the *pootyest*;—now, finally at the eend, boys, this mixtur' of mine will make a fellar talk as iley as goose-grease,—as sharp as lightnin', and as *per*-suadin' as a young gal at a quiltin', so don't spar it while it lasts, and the candidates kin drink furst, 'cause they've got to do the talkin'!"

Having finished his charge he filled the tin cup full of whiskey, put in a handful of brown sugar, and with his forefinger stirred up the sweetening, then surveying the canditates he pulled off his cap, remarking, as he did so:

"Old age, allays, afore beauty!—your daddy furst, in course," then holding up the cup he offered a toast, as follows:

"Here is to the string that binds the states; may it never be bit apart by political *rats!*" Then holding up the cup to his head he took a hearty swig, and passed it to the next oldest looking candidate. While they were tasting it, *Sugar* kept up a fire of lingo at them:

—"and with his forefinger stirred up the sweetening."—*Page* 94.

"Pass it along lively, gentle*men*, but don't spar the *fluid*. You can't help tellin' truth arter you've swaller'd enough of my mixtur', jest fur this reason, its ben 'stilled in honesty, rectified in truth, and poured out with wisdom! Take a *leetle* drop more," said he to a fastidious candidate, whose stomach turned at thought of the way the "mixtur'" was mixed. "Why, Mister," said *Sugar*, coaxingly.

'Ef you wur a babby, jest new born,
'Twould do you good, this juicy *corn!*'"

"No more, I thank you," said the candidate, drawing back from the proffer.

"*Sugar* winked his eye at some of his cronies, and muttered—"He's got an *a*-ristocracy stomach, and can't go the *native licker*." Then dismissing the candidates he shouted,—"crowd up, constitoo*ents*, into a circle, and let's begin fair—your daddy furst, allays; and mind, no changin' places in the circle to git the sugar in the bottom of the cup. I know you're arter it Tom Williams, but none on your yankeein' round to git the sweetnin'—it's all syrup, fellars, cause *Sugar* made and mixed it. The gals at the frolicks allays git me to prepar' the cordials, 'cause they say I make it mity drinkable. Who next? What *you*, old Ben Dent!—Well, hold your hoss for a minit, and I'll strengthen the tin with a speck more, jest because you can kalkilate the valee of the licker, and do it jestiss!"

Thus chatted *Sugar* as he measured out and sweetened up the contents of his kegs, until all who would drink had taken their share, and then the crowd assembled around the speakers. We need not say that the virtues of each political party were duly set forth to the hearers that follows as a matter of course, candidates dwell upon the strong points of their argument, always. One among them, however, more than his compeers, attracted the attention of our friend *Sugar*, not because he had highly commended the contents of his kegs, but because he painted with truth and feeling the claims of the western *pioneers!* Among these he ranked the veteran Col. Johnson and his compatriots, and as he rehearsed their struggles in defence of their firesides, how they had been trained to war by conflict with the ruthless savage, their homes oft desolated, and their children murdered,—yet still, ever foremost in the fight, and last to retreat, winning the heritage of these broad valleys for their children, against the opposing arm of the red man, though aided by the civilized power of mighty Britain, and her serried cohorts of trained soldiery! We say as he dwelt upon these themes *Sugar's* eye would fire up, and then, at some touching passage of distress dwelt upon by the speaker, tears would course down his rude cheek. When the speaker concluded he wiped his eyes with his hard hand, and said to those around him:—

"That arr true as the yearth!—thar's suthin' like talk in that fellar!—he's the right breed, and his old daddy has told him about them times. So did mine relate 'em to me, how the ony sister I ever had, when a babby had her brains dashed out by one of the red skinned devils! But didn't we pepper them fur it? Didn't I help the old man, afore he grew too weak to hold his shootin' iron, to send a few on 'em off to rub out the account? Well, I *did!—Hey!* and shutting his teeth together he yelled through them the exultation of full vengeance.

The speaking being done, candidates and hearers gathered around old *Sugar*, to hear his comments upon the speeches, and to many inquiries of how he liked them, the old man answered:—

"They were all pooty good, but that tall fellar they call Tom, from St. Louis; *you*, I mean, *stranger*," pointing at the same time to the candidate, "you jest scart up my feelin's to the right pint—you jest made me feel wolfish as when I and old dad war arter the red varmints; and now what'll *you* take? I'm goin' to publicly *de*cline in your favor."

Pouring out a tin full of the liquor, and stirring it as before, he stood upright upon the stump, with a foot on each side of his kegs, and drawing off his cap, toasted:—

"The memory of the western *pioneers!*"

A shout responded to his toast, which echoed far away in the depths of the adjoining forest, and seemed to awaken a response from the spirits of those departed heroes.

"That's the way to sing it out, boys," responded old *Sugar*, "sich a yell as that would *scar* an inimy into ager fits, and make the United States Eagle scream 'Hail Columby.'"

"While you're up, *Sugar*," said one of the crowd, give us a stump speech, yourself."

"Bravo!" shouted an hundred voices, "a speech from *Sugar*."

"Agreed, boys," said the old man, "I'll jest gin you a few words to wind up with, so keep quiet while your daddy's talkin'

'Sum tell it out jest like a song,
I'll gin it to you sweet and strong.'"

The ony objection ever made to me in this arr countr, as a legislatur', was made by the *wimin*, 'cause I war a *bachelor*; and I never told you afore why I *re*-mained in the state of number *one*—no fellar stays single *pre*-meditated, and, in course, a hansum fellar like me, who all the gals declar' to be as enticin' as a jay bird, warn't goin' to stay alone, ef he could help it. I did see a creatur' once, named *Sofy Mason*, up the Cumberland, nigh onto Nashville, Tenne*see*, that I tuk an orful hankerin' arter, and I sot in to lookin' anxious fur martrimony, and gin to go reglar to meetin', and tuk to dressin' tremengeous finified, jest to see ef I could win her good opinion. She did git to lookin' at me, and one day, cumin' from meetin', she was takin' a look at me a kind of shy, jest as a hoss does at suthin' he's scart at, when arter champin' at a distance fur awhile, I sidled up to her and blarted out a few words about the sarmin'—she said yes, but cuss me ef I know whether that wur the right answer or not, and I'm a thinkin' she didn't know then, nuther! Well, we larfed and talked a leetle all the way along to her daddy's, and thar I gin her the best bend I had in me, and raised my bran new hat as peert and *per*lite as a minister, lookin' all the time so enticin' that I sot the gal tremblin'. Her old daddy had a powerful numerous lot of healthy niggers, and lived right adjinin' my place, while on tother side lived Jake Simons—a sneakin', cute varmint, who war wusser than a miser fur stinginess, and no sooner did this cussed sarpint see me sidlin' up to Sofy, than he went to slickin' up, too, and sot himself to work to cut me out. That arr wur a struggle ekill to the battle of Orleans. Furst sum new fixup of Jake's would take her eye, and then I'd sport suthin' that would outshine him, until Jake at last gin in tryin' to outdress me, and sot to thinkin' of suthin' else. Our farms wur jest the same number of acres, and we both owned three niggers apiece. Jake knew that Sofy and her dad kept a sharp eye out fur the main chance, so he thort he'd clar me out by buyin' another nigger; but I jest follor'd suit, and bought one the day arter he got his, so he had no advantage thar; he then got a *cow*, and so did I, and jest about then both on our *pusses* gin out. This put Jake to his wits' eend, and I war a wunderin' what in the yearth he would try next. We stood so, hip and thigh, fur about two weeks, both on us talkin' sweet to Sofy, whenever we could git her alone. I thort I seed that Jake, the sneakin' cuss, wur gittin' a mite ahead of me, 'cause his tongue wur so iley; howsever, I didn't let on, but kep a top eye on him. One Sunday mornin' I wur a leetle mite late to meetin', and when I got thar the furst thing I seed war Jake Simons, sittin' close bang up agin Sofy, in the same pew with her daddy! I biled a spell with wrath, and then tarned sour; I could taste myself! Thar they wur, singin' *himes* out of the same book. Je-e-eminy, fellars, I war so *enormous* mad that the new silk handkercher round my neck lost its color! Arter meetin' out they walked, linked arms, a smilin' and lookin' as pleased as a young couple at thar furst christenin', and Sofy tarned her 'cold shoulder' at me so orful pinted, that I wilted down, and gin up right straight—Jake had her, thar wur no disputin' it! I headed toward home, with my hands as fur in my trowsers pockets as I could push 'em, swarin' all the way that she wur the last one would ever git a chance to rile up my feelin's. Passin' by Jake's plantation I looked over the fence, and thar stood an explanation of the marter, right facin' the road, whar every one passin' could see it—his consarned *cow* was tied to a stake in the gardin', *with a most promisin' calf alongside of her!* That *calf* jest soured my milk, and made Sofy think, that a fellar who war allays gittin' ahead like Jake, wur a right smart chance for a lively husband!"

A shout of laughter here drowned *Sugar's* voice, and as soon as silence was restored he added, in a solemn tone, with one eye shut, and his forefinger pointing at his auditory:—

"What is a cussed sight wusser than his gittin' Sofy war the fact, that he *borrowed that calf the night before from Dick Harkley!* Arter the varmint got Sofy hitched, he told the joke all over the settle*ment*, and the boys never seed me arterwards that they didn't *b-a-h* at me fur lettin' a *calf* cut me out of a gal's affections. I'd a shot Jake, but I thort it war a free co intry, and the gal had a right to her choice without bein' made a widder, so I jest sold out and travelled! I've allays thort sence then, boys, that *wimin* wur a good deal like *licker*, ef you love 'em too hard thar sure to throw you some way:

'Then here's to *wimin*, then to *licker*,
Thar's nuthin' swimmin' can be slicker!'"

AN EMIGRANT'S PERILS;

OR, A FLYING TICKET ON THE MISSISSIPPI.

THE inexperienced dweller in a quiet home, who has never been tempted to wander from its peaceful precincts, has but a faint idea of the emigrant's troubles, and many may fail to deeply sympathise with Michael O'Reily, the subject of our sketch; but there are those who have mingled in the perilous tide, and can knowingly speak of its dangers. "Maybe," as Michael would say, "it's mesilf that has had a full peck measure of thim, barrin' what I injayneously iscaped."

Michael's brother, Patrick, had induced him to quit the little cottage and *pratie patch* on the green sod, for a home where "goold" flowed up the rivers. At the time we encountered him he had reached the spot where "a great man intirely," had prophesied this shiny metal would flow to, and he but waited to reach Patrick's home on the Missouri river, to set a net in the stream and catch his share. As he and Mrs. O'R., who was well, but, naturally enough, "wakely," were seated on the boat, considering how they could get further up stream, a steamboat runner came to their aid, and forthwith made every necessary arrangement for taking them safe. Michael's mind being at ease about that matter, he ventured to indulge in a whiff of the pipe, when he was accosted by another of the off-in-twenty-minutes agents.

"Passage up the Missouri, sir?" inquires the runner.

"Yis, I'm goin' wid ye's," says Michael, "sure wan uv your boys *ingaged* me a minnit ago."

The runner perceiving in a moment that a rival had encountered Michael, resolved to *do* the aforesaid rival out of his passenger, and accordingly hurried him off to his own boat, by telling him that *steam was up!*

The "*done*" runner, on returning and finding his passenger off, suspected that the rival boat had secured him, and ventured upon the "terror experiment" to win him back. Michael instantly recognised his first friend, and saluted him with—

"I'm here, ye see!"

"Yes, but you've got yourself into a kingdom-come snarl, if you only know'd it, without half tryin'."

Twist the *snarl* which way Michael would, it sounded unpleasantly, and he ventured to inquire—

"Its what did ye say kind of *snarl*, I was in?"

"I only just want to open your peepers to the fact, of having been trapped on board an old boat, *fully insured*, with a desperate shaky 'scape-pipe, and engaged to be blow'd up this trip ; so good by old fellow, you're ticketed."

"Och! if she's *fully insured*, all's right," says Michael, whispering safety to his heart, "and the boy that I came wid, says she can run up a tree if there's a dhrap of wather on it."

"If she don't run *up* a tree," was the reply, "she'll be sure to run *agin* a snaggy one, and then, I predicate, some of her passengers 'll be blow'd tree high, so you're in for it, old hoss! Good by,—I say, if you should see my old uncle *down thar*," pointing at the same time significantly to the rushing river, "the one I mean who didn't leave me any money, tell him for me, as he's gone to the d—l, to shake himself—will you?" and after delivering himself of this *soothing* request, he vanished, leaving Michael fancying himself astride of a 'scape pipe riding over tree tops, rocket fashion.

"Och sorra the day I iver put fut among sich haythins!" soliloquised Michael, "to talk of a man's bein' blown to *smithereens*, as if it were but a gintle rap wid a shillaleh—faith its out uv this I'll be immigratin' quicker than you could peel a pratie," and forthwith he proceeded to move, with all possible haste, his stock of worldly effects; observing which the runner, who had awoke his fears, shouted out as a *quickener*, "don't forget uncle, for he would think it dreadful mean, if I didn't send word by somebody I knew was *goin' direct*."

"Leave that luggage alone," savagely shouted the mate, "you can't leave this boat—you're *engaged*."

"Thrue for ye's," says Michael in a doleful tone, "be dad I was *omadhaun* enough to do that same, and ye's can blow me up when iver you're a mind to."

"We don't blow her up," says the mate, "until the downward trip, unless some gentleman's requested it in his bargain; if you've got a *flying ticket* we are bound to accommodate you," and just at that moment, *whiz* went a steam-cock.

"Be aisy for the Lord's sake," shouted Michael, "blow her up for the gintleman comin' down; as I'm not used to it, I might fall awkwardly in some man's apple orchard and desthroy a *peach* tree—d'ye mind."

Having been assured that all was safe, and that by express desire the blowing up was deferred, he took his seat at the stern. As the shades of evening gathered around the boat and over the waters, the steamer pushed from her moorings,—the last we saw of Michael he was holding in one hand a small string of beads, with a rosary attached, while the other grasped the painter of the jolly-boat towing astern, and his eye with a doubtful, but resigned expression, was firmly fixed on the shaky *'scape-pipe.*

FUN WITH A "BAR."

A NIGHT ADVENTURE ON THE MISSOURI.

At the head of a ravine on the border of the river Platte, one bright night in June, was gathered a party of Missouri hunters, who were encamped after a day's chase for buffalo. The evening's repast was over, and as they stretched themselves in easy attitudes around their stack of rifles, each looked at the other with a kind of questioning expression, of whether it should be *sleep* or a *yarn?* The bright moon, with full round face, streamed down into their midst, and sprinkled her silvery sheen over shrub and flower, investing night in those vast solitudes with a strange charm which forbid sleep, and with common consent they raised themselves into a sitting posture and proposed a "talk," as the red skins say. Dan Elkhorn was the leader of the party, and all knew his store of adventure inexhaustible, so a unanimous call was made upon Dan for a story. "Come, Dan," cried a crony, "give us something to laugh at, and let us break this silence, which seems to breed a spirit of melancholy—stir us up, old fellow, do!"

Dan pulled his long knife out of his belt, and laying it before him, smoothed back his long grey hair. He was a genuine specimen of the hardy American mountaineer,—like the Indian, he dressed in deer skins and wore the moccason, while every seam in his iron countenance told of 'scapes and peril. Seeing that all were attention he commenced—

"Well, draw up closer, boys, so I shan't have to holler, 'cause breth is gittin' kind a short with me now, and I want to pacel it out to last pretty strong till the wind-up hunt. You, Mike, keep your eye skinned for Ingins, 'cause ef we git deep in a yarn here, without a top eye open, the cussed varmints 'll pop on us unawars, and be stickin' some of thur quills in us—nothin' like havin' your eye open and insterments ready. I've a big idea to gin you an account of some fun I had with an old *bar*, on the Missouri, when I was a younker, and considerably more spry than I am jest now. I want to tell you fust, boys, that bars are knowin' animals, and they kin jest tell a younker of the human kind as easily as they kin a small pig from the old sow;—they don't fool with me now, for they've got to *know me!*

"Well, old Alic Dennison, a neighbour of mine on the Missouri, had bin about two years up in the mountains, and when he came home he gin a treat to all the fellars within thirty miles of him—that was jest seven families—and among 'em, in course, I got an invite. Alic and I had sot our cabins on opposite sides of the drink, near enough to see each other, and a red skin, ef he'd come on a scalp visit, would a bin diskivered by either. When Alic's frolic was to cum off, I was on hand, sartain. About evenin' I got my small dug-out, and fixin' my rifle carefully in the fore eend, and stickin' my knife in the edge whar it would be handy, I jest paddled over the drink.

A little above our location thar wur a bend in the

stream which a kind a turned the drift tother eend up, and planted them about the spot between our cabins—snags and sawyers, jest thar, wur dreadful plenty, and it took mity nice padlin' to git across without tiltin'; howsever, I slid atween 'em, sarpentine fashion, and got over clar as a pet coon. Thar wur considerable folks at Alic's, fur some of the families in them diggins had about twenty in number, and the gals among 'em warn't any on your pigeon creaturs, that a fellar dassent tech fur fear of spilin' 'em, but raal scrougers—any on 'em over fourteen could lick a *bar*, easy. My decided opinion jest now is, that thur never was a grittyer crowd congregated before on that stream, and sich other dancin' and drinkin' and eatin' *bar* steaks, and corn dodger, and huggin' the gals, don't happen but once in a fellar's lifetime, and scarcely that often. Old Alic had a darter Molly, that war the most enticin', gizzard-ticklin', heart-distressin' *feline* creatur that ever made a fellar git owdacious, and I seed Tom Sellers cavortin' round her like a young buffalo—he was puttin' in the biggest kind a licks in the way of courtin', and between her eyes and the sweetened whiskey he'd drank, you'd a thought the fellar would a bursted. Jest to make matters lively, I headed up alongside of Molly, and shyed a few soft things at her, sech as askin' how she liked bar steaks cooked, and if Jim Tarrant warn't equal in the elbow to a mad *panter's* tail, when he war fiddlin' that last reel, and sech amusin' light conversation. Well, boys, Tom started swellin' *instanter*. He tried to draw her attention from me; but I got talkin' about some new improvements I war contemplatin' about my cabin, and the cow I expected up from St. Louis, 'sides lonely feelins I'd bin havin' lately, and

Tom couldn't git in a show of talk, edgeways. Didn't he git mad?—wur you ever near enough to a panter when his *har* riz with wrath? Well, ef you have, you can create some idea of Tom's state of mind, and how electricity, from liquor and love, run out to the eends of his head kiverin'. It wur easy to see he wur a gittin' dangerous, so I slid off and left him alone with the gal. Arter I got a talkin' to another one of the settlers' young women, Molly kept lookin' at me, and every now and then sayin' somethin' pleasin' across to me, while she warn't payin' any attention to Tom at all. He spread himself into a stiff bow and left her; then movin' across the floor like a wounded deer, he steadied himself on the back of my seat, and lookin' me in the face, says:

"'*Mister* Elkhorn, I shud be strenuously obleeged to you ef you'll step down thar with me by the old persimmen tree.'

"I nodded my head, and told him to trot outside and wait till I got the docyments, and as soon as he moved I sent his old *daddy* to accompany him. I jest informed the old fellar that Tom wanted a fight, and as he was too full of corn juice to cut carefully, I didn't want to take advantage of him. The old man said he was obleeged to me, and moved out. Tom, thinkin' it wur me, staggered ahead of the old man, and I concluded, as it war near mornin', to leave; 'cause I knew when Tom found out his daddy was along with him instead of me, he'd have a fight any how. I acknowledge the corn, boys, that when I started my track warn't anythin' like a *bee-line*;—the sweeten'd whiskey had made me powerful thick-legged; but arter a fashion I got to my dug-out, with nothin' of weapon along in the world but the paddle. Thar war jest enough light to tell that snags wur plenty, and jest enough corn juice inside to make a fellar not care a cuss fur 'em. I felt strong as a hoss, too, and the dug-out hadn't more'n leaped six lengths from the bank afore—*zip—chug—co-souse* I went—the front eend jest lifted itself agin a sawyer and emptied me into the ele*ment!* In about a second I came up bang agin a snag, and I guess I grabbed it sudden, while old Missouri curl'd and purl'd around me as ef she was in a hurry to git to the mouth, so she might muddy the Massissippi. I warn't much skeer'd, but still I didn't jest like to hang on thar till daylight, and I didn't want to make a fuss fur fear they'd say I war skary. I had sot myself on the eend of the snag, and was jest tryin' to cypher out some way of gittin' to shore, when I thought I diskiver'd a fellar sittin' on the bank. At fust, he looked so black in the coat I thought it war Tom Sellers, who'd sot himself down to wait fur a fight:—Tom had on at the frolic a black blanket coat with a velvet collar, and he thought it particularly nice. Arter lookin' at him move about and sit down on his hunkers once or twice, I thought I'd holler to him; but he appeared so dreadful drunk that I didn't expect much help from him.

" 'Tom,' shouted I, 'come out here with a dug-out, and help a fellar off, will you?'

"He sot still, without sayin' a word. 'Well,' says I to him, 'you're meaner than an Ingin! and would bait a trap with your daddy's leggins.' He didn't move fur a spell; at last into the drink he popped, and now, thought I, he *is* mad and *no* dispute. I could see him paddlin' right fur me, and I holler'd to him that I had no insterments, but he didn't say a whisper, ony shoved along the faster. At last up he come agin my snag, and the next minit he reached fur me, and then he tried to fix his teeth into my moccason; so guessin' it war time to do somethin', I jest grabbed fur his muzzle, and I'm blessed, boys, ef it warn't a great *he bar!* The cussed varmint had watched me from the house and seed I had no weapons, and when I upsot he just counted me his'n, and was quietly calculatin' on the bank how he'd best git me out of the water. I had nothin' in the yearth but a small fancy pen knife, but I stuck that in him so quick that he let me go, and while he swam for one snag I reached for another. I never heerd a bar laugh out loud afore, but I'm a sucker ef he didn't snigger twice at the way he rolled me off my log.

"We sot lookin' at one another fur a spell, when I seed the varmint gittin' ready to call on me agin, and in about a second more off he dropped, and strait he took a shute for my location. As he came up close to me I slit his ear with the small blade, and he got mad; but jest as he was circling round me to git a good hold, I dropped on to his hinder eend and grabbed his har, and I guess I made him move fur shore a leetle faster than a steam boat—my little blade kept him dreadful *itchy*. Well, the fun of the thing wur, boys, as soon as the varmint teched shore, he turned right round on me, and I'm cussed if I hadn't to turn round, too, and scratch for the snag agin! with that consarned *bar* feelin' my legs with his paw every stroke I war makin' to git away from him! I got a little skary, now, and a good deal mad, fur thar the varmint war a waitin' for me, and whinin' as ef he had been ill-treated, and thar I wur perched up on a sawyer, bobbin' up and down in the water. At last I sot a hollerin' and kept on at it, and hollered louder, until I seed some one cum from the house, and singin' out agin they answered me. I asked who it war, and found that it war Molly, old Alic's darter; so I gin her a description of my siteaytion, and she war into a dug-out in a minit, and paddlin' towards me. I believe I said wonce, boys, that bars wur knowin' critters, but ef thar's anythin' true on this yearth, it's the fact, that this consarned animal had made up his mind to upsot that gal, and I'm blessed ef he didn't jest as cute as ef he'd bin human! Startin' from his snag he swam to the dug-out, put up both paws, and over it went—over went Molly into the stream, and off slid Mister *bar*, laffin' out *loud!* as I'm a white man.

"I seized Molly as she came floatin' towards me, and stuck her upon my sawyer, while I started for an adjinin' snag. I could hear Molly grittin' her teeth, she war so bilin' mad, and jest as soon as she could git breath, she hollered to me to be sure I never rested till I killed that varmint. I swore on that snag that I'd grow thin chasin' the critter, and she seemed to git pacified. Well, thar we wur, in the stream, and it a leetle too rough to swim in easy, so we had to sing out for help, and I yelled till I war nigh onto hoarse, afore anythin' livin' stirred about the house; at last, nigger Jake came down to the edge of the river, jest as day was breakin', and puttin' his hand over his eyes, he hollers—

"'Why, Massa Dan, is dat you wot's been hollowin' eber so long for somebody!'

"'You've jest took the notion to cum see, have you, you lazy nigger—now git a dug-out and come out here and git your missus and me off these snags, and do it quick, too, or I'll make *you* holler!'

"'What, Missus dar, *too!*' shouted the nigger, 'well, dat's funny—de Lor!' and off the cussed blueskin started fur the house, and in a few minits all that could gethered out to see us and laugh at our water locations.

"I had bin gittin' riled by degrees, and now was at a dangerous pint—the steam began to rise off on me till thar wur a small fog above my head, and as the half drunken varmints roared a laffin, and cracked their jokes about our courtin' in the middle of the drink, I got awful excited. 'I'll make ribbons of every man among you,' says I, 'when I git whar thar's a chance to fight.' And then the cussed crew roared the louder. Tom Sellers yelled out that we'd bin tryin' to *elope*, and this made Molly mad,—her daddy got a little mad, too, and I bein' already mad, thar wur a wrathy trio on us, and the old fellow said, ef he thought I'd been playin' a two-faced game, and bitin' his friendship like a pizen varmint, he'd drop me off the log I wur on with a ball from his rifle. I jest told him to fire away and be d—d, for I wur wore out a patience. Some of the boys held him, while others got the dug-out and came to our assistance. I jest got them to drop me on my side of the river, and to send over my rifle, and as soon as it war on hand I onloosed my dog Yelp, and started to wipe out my disgrace.

"That infernal bar, as soon as he'd tossed Molly in the stream, started for the woods; but, as ef he had reasoned on the chances, the varmint came to the conclusion that he couldn't git away, and so got up into a crotch of a low tree, about a quarter of a mile from my cabin. Old Yelp smelled him, and as soon as I clapped peeper on him I let sliver, when the varmint dropped like a log,—I went to him and found he'd bin dead for an nour. My little blade couldn't a killed him, so it's my opinion, clearly entertained, that the owdacious varmint, knowin' I'd kill him for his trick, jest climbed up thar whar I could easy find him, and died to spite me!

"His hide, and hard swearin', got me and Molly out of our elopin' scrape, and the lickin' I gin Tom Sellers that spring has made us good friends ever sence. He don't wonce ventur' to say anythin' about that *bar scrape*, without my permission!"

TELEGRAPHING AN EXPRESS.

A NIGHT'S ADVENTURE IN THE AMERICAN BOTTOM.

THE great struggles to obtain early news in the east, between the proprietors of daily journals, has infused a spirit of rivalry in their western brethren, and *they* have been of late, prating all along the Mississippi valley, about expresses to Washington, railroads to Oregon, regular lines to California, telegraphs connecting St. Louis with the east, &c., and sundry other new-fangled methods of getting ahead of time. We do not much wonder at it, for this is the age of expresses, and the man who lingers along in the old "sure-and-easy" method, is certain to be lost sight of in the rapid whirl of the new order of things. In the matter of *news*, now-a-days, it is not news unless *expressed*, and we hesitate not to say that the President's message, received in the old fashioned wait-till-you-get-it manner, would not be read with interest.

At St. Louis, on the night of the 17th of December, the *President's message* was expected in town, and many were the suspicious rumours in circulation, about private expresses, magnetic telegraphs, and "enormous" arrangements to spread the intelligence with rapidity. Every body knew that the old slow-and-easy line through Illinois would be along sometime that night, and allowing it ten days from Washington to the Mississippi, it was very probable that among its contents would be found a copy of that important document. Col. K., a veteran conducter of the city press, called a few of his boys together, that evening, and quietly remarked to them:—

"Boys, that terrapin team will arrive to night on the other side of the river with the message, and as it generally remains there until next morning, unless we can persuade the driver to cross the river, we will get no message until to morrow, so I wish you to start as an express, and see if you can't coax him to cross.—Use the *persuasive*, liberally, but bring him and the mail-bags, *anyhow!*"

Orders were positive, and a "team" of three started to execute the Colonel's orders. The river was a sheet of solid ice, upon which the full moon poured down a flood of radiance. Across the ice they dashed, gained the Illinois side, and chartering a wagon and horses belonging to a couple of *suckers*, started to meet the stage. The drivers of this *express* were dubious about taking their passengers, because they would not disclose where they wished to go. "Keep dark!" said one. "Mum is the word!" said the other. "They intend to steal sum *gal* on the road," whispered one sucker to his friend.

"Well, they've got a cussed poor taste, fur I'll swar tnar aint anythin' on this yeur road to the bluff wuth shucks, 'cept Nancy Birch, and her temper would tarn the stomic of the d—l." In the course of a few minutes one express passenger remarked to his companion, "We'll meet the *stage* this side of the brick house." "Certain," was his friend's reply. "It's out now," said the biggest sucker, "thar goin' to *rob* the mail," and he cast a fearful glance over his shoulder to see if they had pistols in their hands. The stage was now heard lumbering along, and in a few minutes they met, when out dashed the *expresses*. "Stop!" cried one, to the driver—up mounted another to the side of the stage. "I'm d—d, gentle*men*, ef we belong to that arr crowd!" screamed the sucker driver, "I'll jest swar on a stack of bibles, that them fellars ony hired our team."

The express who mounted the side of the stage, thinking he might obtain a copy from some passenger, thrust his head through the door, and finding one "insider" he demanded:—

"Have you got a *message?*"

"Dake all mit you, mine Got!" exclaimed a German passenger in answer, "but dont gill de fader of dirteen little babys,"—at the same time he handed his wallet to the express messenger.

"To the d—l with your old leather, give me a *message paper!*" shouted the *express*.

"May I go to der *duyvel*, if ish got any oder baper but *Indiana!*" exclaimed the Dutchman, still holding forth his wallet.

The driver now informed them that he had the message along, but "he'd jest see them and the city of St. Louis in h—l, afore they'd git him two steps further than the law *per*vided he should go," and that was to the Illinois side of the river. He said this so *bitter*, that the chance looked hopeless for moving him, bu one of the boys, with a tongue "iley as a sarpint,' quiet as a mole, and civil as a pill pedlar, climbed up on the seat beside him, and placing himself in a good position, he commenced whispering close to the ear of the driver, and Eve never yielded as easily to the serpent's temptation, as the mail driver now began to melt under the soft whisper floating around him.

"You said it would be *hot!*" exclaimed the driver.

"I did," replied the whisper, "and lots of it, besides a dollar under the pitcher of punch, and sundry comfortable fixens around it."

"Don't say any more," said the driver, "that's jest the kind of *snap* I want to git into to night." So, putting up his horses he shouldered the mail bags, and across to St. Louis the party travelled.

The proprietors of the anxious city journals, alarmed at the delay of the *express*, resolved to despatch *telegraphs* in search of them; and, having charged *three* with the *electric fluid*, off they started—and Morse's invention aint a beginning to the way the St. Louis specimens travelled. Across the ice—slap—dash— up the side of the ferry boat, and up the hill. Here were collected about fifty Illinois market wagons, and a corresponding number of *suckers*. A group of these latter were gathered around a large fire, discussing the probability of being able to cross the ice to St. Louis, on the succeeding day. A *telegraph* inquired of one of these, if he had seen anything of the *express*. "No, I haint," says he, "but I hev got first rate butter, at two bitts a pound!" "*Melt* your butter!" shouted an indignant telegraph. "Come and show us the road out to Pap's house, captain," said another. The marketeer started a few rods with him, and then, as if a sudden thought hit him, looked at the telegraph gent, and, pointing his finger at him, he slowly remarked—"No you don't *hoss!* I jest see right through you." "Why, you fool, don't you see by my appearance that I am a gentleman?" inquired *telegraph.* The sucker marketeer drew off a few paces, to be ready to run, and then shouted—"Yes, I've seen jest sich gentleman fellars as *you* in the *penitentiary!*" and off he dashed, congratulating himself on his escape from robbery.

Away went the *telegraphs* again, heading for Pap's house, a stopping place about one mile from the ferry, and while one led the way, the other two, wishing to slip him, hid on the road-side, but the rival telegraph seated himself in the road to wait for the appearance of his company. As there was no way, in the clear moonlight, to get round him unobserved, they came out and again started. Now for it!—best man at Pap's first! Away they started, "lickety-click," and arrived at the winning-post within touching distance of each other. After rapping up the bar-keeper they seated themselves by the stove, leisurely warmed up, and then inquired how soon they expected the stage along. "*It passed here with the message, full twenty minutes ago!*" was the answer.

Clear the track!—*hey!*—here was news. Three important aids of two printing establishments, two miles from their offices, and the message *there!* Now commenced a *stampede* unknown to *Fashion*—down to the river—on to the ice;—pit—pat—pat—pit—slip—slide—bang!—and down he goes "up, boys, and at it again." The island was reached in safety. Here was a dangerous gap, at which stood a foot passenger afraid to cross. "Look out," he shouted, "you'll *get* in there." "Get *thunder!*—get out of the road!" shouted the foremost—through they dashed—the last sticking his leg through a *feet*, and the city side was gained like a flash of lightning. The leading *telegraph* reached the composing room of an enterprising city paper, just as the foreman was shouting—*proof!*

THE PRE-EMPTION RIGHT;

OR, DICK KELSY'S SIGNATURE TO HIS LAND CLAIM.

DICK KELSY was one of the earliest settlers in the Upper Missouri country, and a more open-hearted or careless son of Kentucky, never squatted in the "Far West." He had wandered from his parent state more for a change of location than any desire to improve his condition, and if a spot offered easy hunting facilities, it mattered not what contingencies were added, Dick "*sot* himself down *thar*." Tall, raw-boned, good-natured and fearless, he betrayed no ambition to excel, except in his rifle, and the settlers generally conceded that his "shooting-iron" *was* particularly *certain!* A spot upon one of the tributaries of the Missouri won Dick's heart at first sight—it bordered upon a beautiful stream;—had a far spreading prairie, skirted by a fine grove of timber, for a landscape, and abounded with all sorts of game, from a prairie fowl to an *Indian*. Here Dick built his cabin, beneath the shadow of his own *cotton* tree, and he used to tell his neighbours that nature had, after practising on the rest of creation, spread her finishing touches on his claim. Its wild beauty deserved his lavish praise.

In this western habitation our hero held undisturbed sway, his only companion being a negro slave, who was at once his master's attendant and friend. Kelsy and the negro had been raised together, and from association, although so opposite their positions, had imbibed a lasting affection for each other,—each would have freely shed blood in the other's defence. The bonds of servitude were, consequently, moulded into links of friendship and affection, securing to them a feeling of confidence in their lonely habitation in the wilderness. Their nearest neighbours were situated at a small trading settlement, some ten miles distant, where Dick always repaired to exchange his furs for ammunition and other essentials. Here he also learned the news from the far-off seat of government; but the busy world beyond little interested these roving sons of the western forests,—a brush with the *red skins*, or a challenge shooting match, possessed much more interest for them. At length, however, these western pioneers were aroused from their quietude and inactivity by the news that Congress had passed the famous *Pre-emption Law*. As yet none in the region we write of knew its provisions, or, distinctly, what rights it conferred; each squatter, therefore, laid out the bounds of his claim in accordance with his own desire, and stood ready to defend the title against all encroachments. The fever of emigration became an epidemic, and soon that speculating mania, which, in imagination, built fortunes in a day, spread even to the confines of civilization. The axe of the pioneer soon began to startle the wild denizens of the forest, where for ages the hunter alone had disturbed their repose.

One bright morning a *ripple* of the advancing tide, in the persons of two strangers, was discovered by Dick about a quarter of a mile from his cabin, where, apparently, they had rested for the night. The first was a man about middle stature, of a dark swarthy complexion, with an uneasy eye, prominent teeth, and clad in a dilapidated suit of Kentucky jean;—an old chip hat surmounted his figure, and in his right hand he held the sceptre of the pioneer—a *rifle!* His companion was a pale, sickly-looking little woman, clad in a coarse linsey-woolsey gown, and in her hand she held a faded calico sun-bonnet; close by stood a small wagon, with a quilt cover, to which was harnessed a horse, bearing evident marks of long travel and hard fare.

"How are you, strangers?" was Dick's first query. "Judgin' from appearances, you're lookin' out a location."

"Yes," replied the man, in a surly tone, "I've been lookin' all along, but I aint found any yet fit fur a *white man.*"

"Well, you've jest got to the spot now," says Dick. "Creation aint laid out any place prettier, and arter takin' a view of it, you'll say so. You and the missus better go up to my cabin and rest till you can take a good look at its best *pints*, and I predicate you'll come to a conclusion."

"Well, guess I'll stay a spell," was the stranger's response, and following Dick, he was introduced beneath the Kentuckian's hospitable roof, after which Dick started to the settlement for some notions with which to entertain them more comfortably. On his arrival the whole conversation at the settlement was the *pre-emption act*, and during the debate on its merits, he mentioned the "new arrival" in his neighbourhood, of the strangers They had passed through the settlement, and as all new comers are a subject of interest, various opinions were expressed in regard to these.

"Judgin' from that stranger's frontispiece," said one, "I shouldn't like him fur a near neighbour?"

"He's rayther a sour lookin' customer," added another; "and how dreadful poorly his wife looks."

"I've invited him to locate near me," remarked Kelsy, "and I can't say he's got a very pleasin' look; but the rough shell may have a good kernel, boys."

After providing necessaries, Dick gave the settlers an invitation to come up and help the stranger to raise a cabin. All agreed to be *thar* on the next Saturday, and homeward he started. On his arrival, Sam was cooking the evening meal of wild gåme and corn bread, all the time expatiating to the guests what a good man "Massa Dick" was, and particularly impressing upon their minds that he, (Sam,) was "Massa Dick's 'strordinary niggah!" Sam's efforts at amusement failed upon the strangers, for one was quietly weeping, while the other wore a scowl of anger. Dick noticed their looks on entering, and endeavoured to cheer them—

"Don't look down hearted, strangers," said he, "you aint *among* Ingins ef you are *near* 'em—thar aint a spot in the universal yearth calkilated to make you feel better than whar you are now. Sam and me never felt bad sence we located here,—only when the Ingins penned us in the cabin fur three days, while all our *bar meat* was hangin' on the outside."

"It's this cussed woman," answered the stranger,

"that makes me feel bad—she's etarnally whimperin' about bein' so fur from home—I wish she was in h–ll!"

"Stop that, stranger," said Dick, in a determined tone; "the love I have for an old Kentucky mother won't permit me to see or hear one of her sex abused beneath my cabin roof, ef it is in the wilderness,—I don't like red skins, none of 'em, but even a *squaw* couldn't be abused here!"

"Well, I'm done," was the reply. "I'll git a cabin of my own, and then I guess I'll do as I please."

"No you won't," said Dick; "ef you stay in these diggins and abuse her, you're in a hotter place than whar you jest now wished her."

It may be supposed that the host and his guest retired, the first night of their meeting, with no favourable impression of each other; and while Sam and his master were making all right for the night, the former ventured to remark—

"Dar aint much good in *dat* white man, Massa Dick."

"Not a *heap*, Sam," was his master's reply; "but he shan't pisin us long with his company;" and with this comfortable resolve they turned in for the night.

At daylight Dick started out with his rifle on his arm, to observe the foot-prints around his dwelling, and note whether they were biped or quadruped, the close proximity of the Indian tribes and their frequent thefts, making caution and care necessary to preserve, not only property, but life. As he was returning to his cabin a *scream* startled him from his careless gait—it was a new sound in that wilderness; and many a day had passed since Dick heard anything akin to it. He started forward with a bound, convulsively clutching his rifle, while his blood urged into rapid action by the movement, was again forced back to his heart, chilled by another fearful scream of a woman in distress. In a moment he emerged from the strip of woods, within view of his cabin, and there beheld the stranger with his arm raised to strike; fronting him stood Sam, poising a large hunting knife in defence, while upon the other arm of the muscular negro, hung the trembling form of the stranger's sickly wife. A few moments and Dick was beside the combatants, inquiring the cause of their hostile attitude. When Sam informed him that the stranger had twice, with his fist, felled the woman to the earth, his rifle raised instinctively to his shoulder, as if justice demanded instant and dreadful punishment for such a dastard act. Dick slowly remarked, as he directed his aim—

"I'll sarve you out, you infernal *savage!*"

The stricken wife observing the action, threw herself before the weapon, imploring the enraged host to spare her husband's life.

"Well, woman is woman," soliloquised Dick; "for they'll stick to the devil, ef they ever take a notion to him. If you have the least hankerin' arter the mean varmint, in course I'll let him *slide;* but he must clar out of my diggins—I can't be near whar anythin' of his breed grows,—so arter breakfast we'll separate."

When the morning meal was ended, the stranger drew up his wagon, thrust his companion into it, and sullenly departed, muttering a threatening farewell.

"God help that poor creatur," said Dick, as his late guests disappeared from view, "*she's got a hard row to hoe*, and as for that sarpent with her, he'd better keep out of my tracks. I should be mightily tempted to sarch

"I'll sarve you out, you infernal savage."—*Page* 122.

his carcass to see ef he had a heart in it. Sam," continued he, "*you're* a nigger, but thar's more real white man under your black skin than could be found in an acre of such varmints as that *sucker*. Give me your fist, old fellar; while Dick Kelsy's got anythin' in this world, you shall share it!"

While this bond of closer friendship was being formed between master and slave, malice was holding her revel in the heart of their late guest. He had observed Dick's love for the spot where he had squatted, and judging rightly that he had neglected to file his claim to it in the Land Office, he stopped a short distance below him, intending to remain, and, if possible gain possession of it. Kelsy had his dislike for the stranger increased by finding him remain on his section, and he ordered him to leave forthwith. The stranger gave as an excuse, that his wife was so sick that she couldn't travel, and ended with a request that he would let him erect a hut to shelter her, while he went in search of a permanent location. In pity for *her*, Dick consented, and the stranger proceeded to prepare timber for a small cabin. The following Saturday the neighbors gathered, and by nightfall placed a roof over their heads, kindly supplied them with some necessaries, and left, each more confirmed in his dislike for the stranger. The next morning he started off, as many supposed, never to return; the natural kindness of the settlers was immediately manifested towards his wife, and nothing that would conduce to her comfort, was lacking in the cabin of this heart-broken woman.

After the lapse of several days, contrary to all expectation, the stranger returned, and a visible change was manifested in his manner—his surliness assumed a more impudent and offensive character, and on receiving a further intimation that it was time he was *moving*, he insolently told Dick to "clear out," himself, for that he, (the stranger,) was the rightful owner of the claim. Dick laughed at him, and told him to be off quietly, that his carcass was safe while that woman clung to him.

Kelsy was laughing next day, down at the settlement, as he related the stranger's words, and described his insolent bearing; but his smile of scorn was turned to a frown of wrath, when the Land Agent, who happened to hear him, informed the unsuspecting squatter, that the stranger had, indeed, entered the claim his cabin was upon. Dick, on hearing this news, shivered the bottle in his hand to atoms, and drawing his breath through his teeth until it fairly whistled, he remarked—

"That stranger may have *some* of my claim, but his share shall be my *signature to the title*."

The sun was fast sinking when Dick started home, rather limber from the effects of wrath and liquor. Having resigned himself to the care of his horse, he swung from side to side, in a state of dozing unconsciousness. When he neared his cabin, it had become pitch dark, to which, if possible, the woods bordering his claim, added a gloomier shade. The instant his horse entered beneath the foliage, a sharp pain shot through the side of the rider, so acute as to wake his powers suddenly into full consciousness. The spring he made in the saddle startled his horse forward into a rapid gait, and in an instant more, a sickly sensation robbed him of all consciousness. When he opened his eyes with returning animation, his look fell upon his faithful slave, who was bending, with an anxious countenance, over the rude couch of his master.

"Bress God! Massa Dick, you knows Sam, your ole nigga—I sees you does—dars life in you yet, massa,—dar is, but dis poor nigga had amost gib you up, for sartain!"

An unseen hand had, in the darkness, plunged a knife into Dick's body, as he entered the wood; he had clung to his horse's mane, until the animal stopped at his cabin door, where Sam, waiting for his master, had caught his bleeding and unconscious body in his arms as it fell reeling from the saddle. The faithful negro had staunched the blood, and applied every restorative his rude knowledge could devise; but it was long ere the eyes he so loved opened to the recollection of past events and present injury.

"That was a foul dig in the ribs, Sam," murmured his exhausted master; "but ef I don't trail up the sarpint and pull his sting out, it'll be because I and that ar old rifle of mine has to part company!"

The natural strength of the patient, together with Sam's careful nursing, soon restored him to his legs, and a few days' gentle exercise imparted strength enough to his frame to support the weight of his rifle. A fixed resolve to trace the assassin added a severe cast to Dick's pale features—Sam, as he observed him, quietly shook his head, with the remark—

"Ah, ah! Massa Dick's soon goin' Ingin huntin'—*sure!*"

One morning, early, Kelsy ordered Sam to saddle his horse, and proceeded himself to clean his rifle; with more than usual care he adjusted each particular of his accoutrements, and started off to the settlement, taking the road leading by his neighbor's cabin. On his arrival, he gathered a few of his cronies together, who all knew of the dastardly attempt on his life, and imparted to them a scheme he had been maturing, for discovering if the stranger was the "stabber in the dark,"—which few seemed to doubt, but of which he wished to be certain.

As the sun inclined to the west, Kelsy made preparation for return, and changing his dress for a suit belonging to one of his friends, he stuffed his own with straw, surmounted the figure with his fur cap, and mounted it upon his horse before him, where it was secured to the saddle; four of his friends accompanied him, and thus prepared, they bent their course towards Dick's cabin. Night set in while they were on their march, and soon the moon rose, casting her soft light over a prairie landscape, as beautiful as ever the eye of man rested upon. It was a western scene of wild and picturesque loveliness, grand in its vastness of extent, and rich in its yet hidden resources. Its lonely quietude was calculated to subdue the wild passions which throbbed in the hearts of those who now broke its stillness; but a glance at the firm features of the party, proved that its beauty was unheeded by them as they swept onward to the dread business of their march. When within a mile of Dick's habitation, they halted in a secluded hollow, where they resigned their horses to the care of one of the party, with instructions to turn Kelsey's horse loose about the time he supposed they, by a circuitous route, on foot, had reached the woods, and when he heard a shot, to follow with their other horses. Dick and his companions stole unperceived beneath the shadow of the wood, and cautiously approached the trail leading to his cabin; ere they had reached the spot, however, one of the party descried the horse leisurely wending his way across a strip of prairie, the figure seated upon his back swaying from side to side, so like his owner when "half sprung," that they could with difficulty suppress a laugh. The sound of the horse's hoofs brought from concealment another figure, whose form was indistinctly visible, emerging from behind a thick covert; and the excitement of the moment, at thus having securely trapped the offender, had almost discovered them—their game, however, was too intent on his purpose, or he would have heard the slight exclamation which burst from the lips of one of the party. Moving stealthily to a good position he awaited horse and rider, and taking deliberate aim, *fired.* No movement of the figure indicated a *hit*, and the party could hear his exclamation of disappointment. The horse sauntered along undisturbed by the report, perceiving which, the assassin hastily reloaded, while Dick and his friends crept up unperceived almost to his side. Raising his rifle again, he steadily poised his aim, and pulled the trigger—erect the figure held its place, and resting his rifle upon the ground, he exclaimed—

"I've *hit* him, or he's the *devil himself!*"

"I guess its the old gentle*man* come for you, stranger," said Dick, as he snatched the rifle from his hand, and the whole party closed in a circle round him.

The detected squatter looked paralyzed—his tongue refused its office, while his form, quivering with apprehension, could scarcely keep erect, and his usually cold, uneasy eyes seemed fixed balls of light, so dreadful were they in their expression of coward fear. The party proposed to settle his business at once, and this movement loosened his tongue—he broke forth in piteous accents of supplication—

"Oh, God! oh, God!" cried he, "you won't kill me—will you?"

"Well," said one of the party, "*we won't do anything else!*"

Kelsy interposed, and suggested that his death be deferred until daylight, in order that the stranger might see how it was done, and be put to sleep respectably. They immediately adjourned to Dick's cabin, where they found Sam holding the straw figure in his arms, and looking in a state of stupor at the horse; he thought his master was "done for;" but great was his joy when the well-known sounds of Kelsy's voice assured him of his safety.

The party seated themselves in a circle in the cabin, with the culprit in the centre, and his shrinking form, trembling with fear, and pallid, imploring countenance, looked most pitiful. As Kelsy gazed upon him the form of his sickly wife seemed to twine her arms around his neck, beseeching as when she before interposed herself between him and death, and the vision of his mind searched out a tender spot in Dick's heart. He resolved to give him a chance of escape, and, therefore, proposed to the party that they should decide by a *game of cards*, whether the stranger should die or be permitted to leave the country. Dick's friends protested against such mercy; but after an earnest appeal from him, in behalf of the woman, they yielded—cards were produced, and one of the party selected to play against the culprit. By Kelsy's entreaty, also, he was allowed the choice of his own game, and he selected *euchre*. All seated themselves closer around the players—breathing seemed almost suspended—a beam of hope lent a slight glow to the pallid countenance of the stranger, while the compressed lips and frowning brow of his antagonist, gave assurance that no mercy would temper his play for this fearful stake. The rest of the party shared his dislike for the culprit, who was looked upon as a common foe, and their flashing eyes were bent upon his swarthy countenance with an expression of deadly hate, which forced out the cold drops of perspiration upon his sickly brow, and sunk his heart with fear. The cards were cut, and the stranger won the *deal*—he breathed with hope—he dealt and turned up the *right bower*—his antagonist *passed*, and the stranger raising the *bower*, bid him play. The hand was soon finished and the stranger counted *two!* His visage lighted up, and he wiped his brow with a feeling of confidence in his luck The next hand the stranger ordered the card up and was *euchered*—they now stood *even*, and he again looked anxious. In the next two hands they successively won, each a single count, and it was the stranger's deal again —he turned up a *king*, and held in his hand the *queen* and *ten of trumps*, together with the *eight of diamonds* and the *king* and *ten of clubs*. His antagonist ordered the *king* up, and as the stranger discarded his *diamond*, a gleam of certain success overspread his visage—the rigid face of his antagonist betrayed no sign of exultation, but his brow, on the contrary, became closer knit into a scowl, which, by his party, was looked upon as a presage of defeat. Dick's friend led the *jack of clubs* —the stranger followed suit with his *ten of clubs*—then came the *ace of trumps*—the stranger paused a moment, and played his *ten spot*—out came the *right bower*, and he yielded his *queen*—the *left* fell before his eyes, and his last *trump*, the *king*, was swept away! At each play his countenance grew more and more ashy in its expression of despair and dread; his lips had lost their color, and his eyes had gained an intenseness of expression that seemed as if they could look into the very soul of the frowning figure before him, and read there his impending doom. For the first time a slight smile played upon the features of Dick's friend as slowly he spread before him the *ace of clubs!* The stranger crushed his *king* within his trembling hands and threw it from him, as he sunk into a state of stupor, the very counterpart of death.

"Your game's up, stranger," coolly remarked the winner; "yes, it's *up*—played very *neat*—but it's up! And you've jest won a *small* patch of Kelsy's claim—about six foot by two, or thereabouts."

The sun had begun to tip the tops of the forest trees, when this exciting contest was ended, and all the party adjourned to the outside, with the doomed stranger in their midst. They moved with silence, for a deed of blood was to be enacted. The law of the wilderness was about to offer up a victim for common safety—the midnight assassin to expiate his guilt upon the spot, and by the hand of him whom he had there endeavored to consign to death.—The music of the morning songsters met no harmonious accord in the hearts of those who now strode amid their melodies—the sweet morning air kissed brows fevered with passion, and the light breeze that played amid the forest grove and skipped innocently across the far spread prairie, was about to bear upon its pinions the shriek of agony. Having arrived at a suitable spot, they bound the culprit to a sapling, and he hung in his bonds already, apparently, bereft of life.

"Stick him up at a hundred yards, boys," said Dick; "ef he is a *snake*, give him a 'small show' for life, and ef I miss him at the first fire we'll let him *slip*."

The culprit aroused on hearing this, and plead for the smallest chance in the world.

"Don't shoot me like a *mad dog!*" he exclaimed, in most piteous accents.

"You're worse, you hound," said his late antagonist; "and if Dick don't wind up your business for you, *I* will."

"Come, boys," continued Dick, "you all know that this old iron's *certain*, so give the varmint this chance—it'll please him, and he'll die off all the easier!"

After some persuasion, Dick's request was acceded to, and the parties took their positions. Life hung, for the culprit, by but a thread, and that thread the will of Kelsy. Slowly the latter raised his rifle, while the party, breathless, intently fixed their eyes upon the victim. Dick's hand began to tremble, and his aim became unsteady, for the sickly form of the stranger's wife again seemed to rise and plead for mercy—he rested his rifle on the ground, without the heart to fire; but, in an instant the vision fled, and his eye fell clear upon the countenance of the stranger; a morning ray lighting up his features, exhibited a gleam of mingled triumph, hatred, hope, and revenge—there was no mistaking its dark expression of contending passions. The pity that had almost unnerved Kelsy and saved his foe, vanished, and raising his rifle sudden as thought, the weapon rung out the stranger's knell. As the ball from its muzzle sped through his brain, a wild shriek arose upon the air, and all was again still—they loosened his bonds, and he fell forward, *dead!*

His remains were consigned to the earth without a tear, even from his companion, to whom the tragedy had been imparted. His cruelties had long since obliterated from *her* heart the last spark of early fondness; all she requested, when the grave had closed over him, was to be sent to her friends in Ohio, which was kindly done by the settlers—Dick bestowing upon her his whole stock of fine furs to defray her expenses.

Kelsy set himself down in undisturbed possession of his claim, and Sam, his faithful slave, often points to the small green mound at the edge of the grove, with the remark—

"Dat's Massa Dick's signature to dis land claim—*dat is!*"

YALLER PLEDGES;

OR, THE FIGHT ABOUT SALLY SPILLMAN.

"It aint natral fur a fellar to tell of his gittin' licked, but I must tell you about that thar fight between me and Jess Stout—it war a screamer, by thunder! and ef I did gin in, it warn't in the course of human natur' to do any how else. That gal *spontenaceously* hankered arter Jess, and besides, he'd piled up the affection in her, by an amazin' long spell of courtin'. I did kinder edge into her likin', and gin to speckelate big on throwin' Jess, but that fight knocked my calculations all to fritters. I'm some in a *bar* fight, and *con*siderable among *panters*, but I warn't no *whar* in that fight with Jess. In course, I'll tell you, boys, so sot yourselves round, and pass along that *corn juice*.

"You see, every time I come up from Lusiane, I found Jess hangin' round that gal, Sally Spillman, lookin' orful sweet, and a fellar couldn't go near her without risin' his dander—he was jealous as a hen with young chickens. I sot my eyes on her, to find out what Jess saw in her so amazin' inticin', and I swar ef a close examination didn't make me yearn arter her like a weaned yearling. She was all sorts of a gal—thar warn't a sprinklin' too much of her—she stuck out all over jest far enough without cushinin'—had an eye that would make a fellar's heart try to get out of his bosom, and then sich *har* ;—her step was as light as a panter's, and her breath sweet as a prairie flower. In my opinion, the mother of all human natur' warn't an atom slicker model; she desarved the pick of a whole creation, and I jest felt that I was made a purpose for her!

"At all the frolicks round the country, down in the Missouri bottom, or up the Osage, Jess was hangin' arter that gal, lookin' *honey* at her, and *pizin* at the fellars who spoke pleasin' to her. I thort I'd try my hand at makin' him oneasy, so one night, at a frolick, I sidled up to her and axed how she wur, and ef that ailin' nigger of her daddy's wur improvin', what 'ud be the probable amount of the old man's tobaccer crop this season, and some other interestin' matters of talk. She said that she was thrivin', as usual, the nigger wur comin' on as well as could be expected, and the old man's crop promised to be purty considerable. Nothin' could be more satisfyin', so I kept on a talkin', and she got a laffin', and Jess begun a scowlin'. I seed he warn't pleased, but I didn't estimate him very tall, so I kept on, got a dancin' with Sally, and ended by kissin' her good by, that night, and makin' Jess jealous as a pet pinter!

"I wur agoin to start to Lusiane next day, with a flat load of tobaccer and other groceries, and afore I went, I thort I'd send a present of my pet 'bar cub' over to Sally, jest to have a sorter hitch on her till I'd git back; so I gits my nigger Jim and gins him the followin' note, with the bar cub, and special directions that he wur to give 'em both to Sally, herself:

"'PANTER CRIK, NEAR BAR DIGGINS,
Juin twenty 4.

"'TO THE CAPTIVATIN' MISS SALLY SPILLMAN:

"'Your tender adorer, Sam Crowder, sends you the followin' fust trofy of a hunt on the Osage; the condition of this *bar* are somethin' like him, the bar are all *fat*, he are all *tenderness!* Hopin' that you will gin up a small corner of your heart to the writer, while he is among the furriners of Lusiane, he will ever remember you, and be sure not to furgit to bring a *pledge of affection* from the sunny south, to bind our openin' loves.

"'Yours, *with* stream, or *agin* it,
"'SAM CROWDER.

"I studdyed that out with considerable difficulty, and writ it with more, and 'stick me on a sand-bar' ef that Jess didn't way-lay Jim and read the note! Maybe it didn't stir up the alluvial bottom of his love fur Sally—the varmint's countenance looked as riled as the old Missouri in a June rise.

"Off I started next day, with my flat, for the imporium of the south, and as I war floating along, I couldn't help turnin' over in my mind what a scrougin smart family the Crowders would be, when Sally and I agreed upon annexation. I jest thort I could see 'young Sam,' the fust boy, standin' on the other eend of the flat, strong as a bar—eye like an Ingin—spry as a catamount—fair as Sally and keen as his daddy—I swar, I yelled rite out, thinkin' on it.

"While I was in this way rollin' in clover, by picturin' what was to be, they wur tarin' my character all to *chitlins* up at home. My perlite note was raisin' a parfect freshet of wrath agin me. That display of larnin', about bringin' home a *pledge of affection*, from the sunny south, most onaccountably oversot my whole family prospects. It wur a stumper to Sally, so she got Jess to explain it, and the way he did it was *enormous*.

"'Why, don't you see,' ses Jess, 'he means to bring you up one of his nigger children, from the south, to *nuss!* Nothing can be plainer—thar aint no other 'pledges of affection' than children, that I know on.'

"Well, I swar ef she didn't believe him.

"'The nasty dog,' ses Sally, 'does he think I'm agoin to *nuss* any of his *yaller pledges*—ef them thar is all he's got to offer, he aint wuth *shucks*, and ef you don't lick him fur his onmannerly note, you aint wuth shucks, nuther.'

"Not dreamin' of the row at home, I was a huntin' through Noo Orlins fur presents fur Sally. I bought a roll of ribbon, a pocket full of lace, and a bran new, shinin' silk parasol, and was comin' along, slow and easy, by the St. Louis Exchange, when I heerd Major Beard cryin' off a lot of field hands. I jest sauntered in as he was puttin' up a picanninny 'yaller gal,' about five years old. The little gal had no mammy livin', and looked sorter sickly, so nobody seemed anxious to git her. I hollered fifty dollars, and the little creatur' brightened up when she seed who was a biddin'; I didn't look like a sugar or cotton planter, and the creatur' seemed glad that I warn't. Some cotton fellar here bid sixty dollars, and she wilted rite down—I thort what a slick present she'd be fur Sally, and how well she'd do to tend the children, so I sung out seventy dollars; she knew my voice, and I could see her eyelids trimble. No sooner did the Major drop the hammer on seventy dollars, than she looked wuth a hundred, she was so pleased at my buyin' her. She was a nice little creatur', but her *har* was oncommon straight.

"I started up home next day, with my purchases, and sich a time as I had on the way. I got dreamin' so strong about bein' married to Sally, that I was etarnally wakin' up huggin' and kissin' the pillows, as ef they wur gals at a huskin'. At last I got home, tickled all to death at my future prospects. I met Jess at the landin'—he gin me a starr, looked at the little yaller gal, and then spread himself with a guffaw, as ef he wur goin' into fits. I riled up a little, but thought thar wur time enough to sarve him out, so I passed on. The fellars in the settle*ment* seemed to be allfired pleased at my gittin' back, fur they kept a grinnin' and bowin' and lookin' at my little yaller gal.

"'Wont you take a little suthin', Sam,' said Jim Belt, the grocery keeper.

"'Not now, I thank you, Jim, ses I.'

"'What, you aint agoin' in fur temperance *pledges*, too, are you?' asked Jim, and then the boys all holler'd as ef they'd bust thar heads.

"'Not ex-a-c-t-ly!' ses I, rather slow, tryin' all the time to find out what the fun war, but I couldn't get it through my kiverin' of *har*, so I gin it up and went home. Next day thar wur to be a campmeetin' down in the bottom, and all the boys and gals wur agoin' to it; so, to make a shine with Sally, I sent over word that I would call that mornin' and bring with me my fust *pledge of affection*, meanin' the parasol, and hoped it would be to her mind both in *textur* and color. Back came this note in anser:

"'KUNE HOLLER, *Juli* 8.

"'Miss Spillman's compliments

"'To Sam Crowder, Esq.; the fust *pledge of his affections* is a little too *yaller*, and the *textur* of its *har* is too tight a curl, and, more'n that, she aint ambitious to hev any of his pledges ef tha wur all *white*.

"'SALLY SPILLMAN.'

"I nigh onto bust with madness!—I could feel every *har* on my head kindlin' at the eend, 'cause I knew sum cussed lie had been told her, and I blamed Jess fur doin' it. I jest swar a bible oath, I'd spile his pictur' so he couldn't enjoy campmeetin' *much;* so next mornin,' bright and airly, I *accidentally* fell in with Jess, goin' arter Sally, with all his Sunday kiverin' on, lookin' as nice as a 'stall fed two year old.' I rite up and asked him what he meant by tellin' lies to the galls about me; that I'd hearn on 'em all over the settle*ment.*

"'I haint told no lie on you,' ses Jess, 'fur what's told, you told yourself—ef you hev *nigger babies* in the south, you needn't insult decent white gals by offerin' to let 'em *nuss* 'em—'

"I didn't wait till he finished afore I hit him, *biff*, alongside of his smeller, and went into him *all-fours*, catamount fashion. The thing had now cum to a windin' up pint—this fight war to eend the matter about Sally, and as I didn't want to gin her up easy, I laid myself out fur a purty long spell. I could soon see by the way Jess went to work that he'd kalculated upon a pretty big *chunk* of a fight, too, so we both began to save ourselves. I had a leetle the advantage of Jess, for he didn't want to spile his Sunday fix-ups, while I didn't care a cuss fur my old boat suit. When I'd grab his trowsers and gin 'em a hitch, he'd ease off, and then I'd lend him a staggerer, which was generally follered by his makin' me fly round like a weazel—cre-*a*-tion, how tough he war!

"While we wur havin' a rite smart time together, nary one of us seed Sally ridin' along down the wagin track, lookin' out fur Jess, but she seed us, hitched her horse, and climbed onto a stump to see the fight out. As I war carfully reachin' fur Jess' ear with my grinders, I heerd her sing out—

"'Tech it ef you *dar!*—you nigger cannibal!'

"Her hollerin' gin Jess an advantage and helped his strength powerfully, fur the next minit I war on my back and him right astraddle on me.

"'*Sock* your teeth into him, Jess!' screamed Sally, and about then, *je-e-e-miny* fellars, I leaped as ef lightnin' had hit me, fur his grinders had met through the flesh she called his attention to. I squirmed, and struggled, and chawed meat, but he held on—I grabbed his new trowsers, and tore them like paper—he was agoin to let go to kiver his coat tails over the torn place, but Sally hollered out agin—

"'Whip the varmint fust and then I'll mend 'em up!'

"I squealed *enough!* rite out—it warn't no use a fightin' agin such odds. Arter Jess let me up, Sally looked at me, and puckered up her mouth as ef she had been eatin' unripe persimmons—

"'*Enough!*' ses she, 'well, may I git ager fits, ef you're fit fur anythin' but to be the father of *yaller pledges!*'"

"*Enough!*" ses she; "Well, may I git ager fits, ef you're fit fur anythin' but to be the father of *yaller pledges!*"—*Page* 138.

GEORGE MUNDAY,

THE HATLESS PROPHET.

This odd character has lately favored the west with a visit, and during two successive evenings he edified audiences, numbering about a thousand persons, in the rotunda of the St. Louis court-house. Some took him for the *Wandering Jew*, and as he inveighed against the evils of these modern days, they looked at him with a feeling of awe. One day opposite the Planter's house, during a military parade, George was engaged selling his edition of the "Advocate of Truth," when a tall hoosier, who had been gazing at him with astonishment for some time, roared out in an immoderate fit of laughter.

"What do you see so funny in me, to laugh at?" inquired George.

"Why, hoss," said the hoosier, "I wur jest a thinkin' ef I'd seed you out in the woods, with all that *har* on, they would a been the d—dest runnin' done by this coon ever seen in them diggins—you're ekill to the *elephant!* and a leetle the *har*-yest small man I've seen *scart* up lately."

A sight at George, on his western tour, has brought to my recollection an anecdote, which entitles him to a place in our collection of odd characters;—it occurred several years since, in Philadelphia, and the writer was an eye witness of the occurrence.

George's favorite neighborhood for "holding forth," was in and about the famous old "State House," where, bare-headed—with unshorn beard, and adorned with a simple wooden cross, he, in a few moments, would collect a crowd. At length the police arrested him, for obstructing the passage, and George was sent to the Alms-House. In a few days, he escaped from the institution, and, boiling with indignation, hastened back to his old haunt, to lay his grievances before the people. Having provided himself with a couple of *gimlets*, he entered the building, raised the large window above the back entrance, and, placing himself on the old-fashioned entablature over the door-way, (the same spot where the Declaration of Independence was read from,) he shut down the window behind him, securing himself from interruption by boring his gimlets through the sash, into the frame. Then, with much solemnity, he proceeded to paraphrase the "Declaration," applying it to his own particular case. The scene was truly ludicrous. Below, was one of the high constables and an assistant policeman, together with a numerous crowd of curious hearers.

"When, in the course of human events"—began George.

"Will you come down from there?" demanded the constable.

"A long train of abuses and takings up without authority,—"

"Aint you a comin'; now?—if you don't I'll *bring* you," threatened authority.

"Our mayor, like the kings of old, set upon us swarms of corrupt and drunken officers to put the prophets of truth into pestilential abodes."

"Now, *do*, George, stop your lingo—that's a good fellow," said the officer, coaxingly, seeing that the usual means of reaching the offender were cut off; "and come down without bother."

"Look up!" shouted the indignant advocate of truth, "look up, you stiff-necked, corrupt son of Belial!—you dog in office!—you, that belch forth the corrupt effluvium of liquid death, commonly styled *rum!—you* are the chief of a band of authorised knaves, composed of evil expounders of the law, otherwise called *pettifoggers*, and certain other rogues in office, who are styled "the police."—You lead captive the senses of the *mayor*, who is as much bridled by your wickedness as the beast of the same name!—you cause him by your false tongues to do evil, but, there *is* a day coming—*there is!* when, at a *bar* where your credit has long since been chalked out, I'll make an *affidavy* will knock you so far into the regions of darkness, that the final trump will sound like a *penny whistle* to your ear!—do you hear that!"

The policeman did hear *that*, but his amiability could stand it no longer; so, procuring a watchman's ladder, he commenced climbing to the prophet, who coolly unscrewed his gimblets, hoisted the window, lifted up his robes, and, shouting "woe to the wicked," beat a successful retreat.

COURTING IN FRENCH HOLLOW.

"Courtin' is all slick enough when every body's agreed, and the gal aint got no mischief in her, but when an extensive family, old maids, cross daddy, and a romantic old mommy, all want to put thur fingers into the young uns dish of sweet doin's, and the gal's fractious besides, why a fellar that's yearnin' arter matrimony is mity likely to git his fires dampened, or bust his biler."

Thus reasoned Tom Bent to a select party of river cronies, who were seated around him upon the boiler deck of a Mississippi steamer, as she sped along one bright night in June, somewhere in the neighborhood of Bayou Teche. The subject was courting, and on that particular question Tom was considered an oracle, for, besides having a strong *penchant* for the fair sex, he had run many risks to ingratiate himself in their affections. Tom was now fast falling into the sear and yellow leaf of bachelorism, and although he had vowed unalterable affection to at least one fair one in each town between the mouth and the rapids, he still remained in unblessed singleness.

"How about that afarr of your'n with old Fecho's gal, in St. Louis, Tom?" inquired one of the circle.

"What, that little French gal?" inquired Tom, with a grin; "well, that thar was a salty scrape, boys, and though the laugh is agin me thar, I'm blessed if I don't gin you the sarcumstince." So Tom squared himself for a yarn, wet his lips with a little corn juice, took a small strip of Missouri weed, and "let out."

"That gal of old Fecho's wur about the pootyest creatur, fur a foreigner, I ever took a *shute* arter; her eyes jest floated about in her head like a star's shadow on a Massissippi wave, and her model was as trim as the steamer Eagle, 'sides, her paddles wur the cleanest shaped fixins that ever propelled anythin' human, and her laugh rung like a challenge bell on a 'fast trip'—it couldn't be beat. She run into my affecshuns, and I couldn't help it. I danced with her at some on the balls in Frenchtown, and thar I gin to edge up and talk tender at her, but she ony laughed at my sweet'nin'. Arter a spell, when I cum it strong about affecshun, and the needcessity of towin' side and side together, she told me that her old daddy wouldn't let her marry an American! Ef I warn't snagged at this, I wouldn't say so. The old fellar wur a sittin' on a bench smokin' and lookin' on at the dance, and I jest wished him a hot berth for a short spell. 'Well, Marie,' said I, 'ef I melt the old man down will you gin in?'

"'Oh,' says she, 'you so vair strong at de vat you call *coax*, I shall not know how to say von leetel no.'

"So havin' fixed it all with her smooth as a full freight and a June rise, I drew up alongside of the old fellar, jest as he had cleared his chimley for a fresh draw of his pipe. Old Fecho had been a mountain trader, was strong timbered, not much the worse fur wear, and looked wicked as a tree'd bear. I fired up and generated an inch or two more steam, and then blew off at him. 'That's an onconscionable slick gal of your'n, Mounseer,' says I, to begin with, and it *did* tickle his fancy to have her cracked up, 'cause he thought her creation's finishin' touch,—so did I! 'Oui, sair,' says old Fecho, 'she vair fine leetel gal, von angel wizout de ving, she is, sair, mine only von *fille*.'

"'Well, she is a *scrouger*,' answered I, 'a parfect high pressure, and no dispute!'

"'Vat you mean by him, eh? vat you call s-c-r-r-r-ouge, eh? vat is he, sair, my leetel gal no vat you call von s-c-r-r-r-ouge, sair!' and here old Fecho went off into a mad fit, jest as ef I'd called her bad names. I tried to put down his 'safety valve,' but he would blow off his wrath, and workin' himself into a parfect freshet of rage, he swore he would take the little gal off home; and I'm blessed ef he didn't. As soon as I eyed the old fellar startin' I got in his wake and follered him, detarmined to find out whar he located, and arter an eternal long windin' through one street arter another, down he dived into French Hollow. Jest as he wur about to enter a house built agin the side of the hill, the old fellar heered my footsteps, and turnin' round in the darkness, he shouted—

"'Ah, ha! von sneak Yankee doodel, vat call my leetel gall von s-c-r-r-r-ouger, I shall cut you all up into von leetel piece vidout von whole.'

"You know, boys, I aint easy skeer'd, but I own up that old fellar did kind a make me skeery; they told sich stories about the way he used to skin Ingins, that I gin to think it was about best to let him have both sides of the channel ef he wanted it, so I didn't darr go to see Marie fur a long spell. One day I felt a strong hankerin', and jest strolled along the holler to git a glimpse on her, and sure enough thar she wur, a leanin' out the winder, smilin' like the mornin' sun on a sleepin' bayou. I sidled up to the house, and asked her ef I darr cum and sit up with her that evenin'. I told her

I was jest fritterin' away all to nothin' thinkin' on her, and a small mite of courtin' would spur me up amazin', and then I gin her sich a look, that she fluttered into consent as easy as a mockin' bird whistles.

"'Oh, *oui*, you shall come sometime dis night, when *mon pere* is gone to de *cabaret;* but you must be vair quiet as von leetel rat, vat dey call de mouse, and go vay before he come back to de *maison.*'

"In course I promised to do jest as she said. I kissed my hand to her, and said *aur ravoir*, as the French say for good by, and then paddled off to wait for night. I felt wuss than oneasy until the time arriv, and when it did git round I gin to crawl all over—I swar I was a leetle skeered. Hows'ever, it warn't manly to back out now when the gal was expectin' me, so I started for the Hollow. I think a darker night was never mixed up and spread over this yearth—you remember, Bill, the night you steered the old Eagle square into the bank at Milliken's bend? well, it wur jest a mite darker than that! A muddy run winds along through the ravine whar the house stands, and I wur particularly near floppin' into it several times. A piece of candle in the winder lighted me to whar the little gall was a waitin', and when I tapped at the door below, she pattered down and piloted me up to the sittin' room, whar we sot down and took a good look at each other. She looked pooty enough to tempt a fellar to bite a piece out on her. I had all sorts of good things made up to say when a chance offered, and here the chance wur, but cuss me ef I could get out the fust mutter. Whether it wur skeer at the idee of the old Frenchman, or a bilin' up of affecshun fur his darter that stuck my throat so tight, I'm unable to swar, but thar I wur, like a boat fast on a sand-bar, blowin' some, but makin' mity little head-way.

"'Vat is de mattair wiz you, Mounseer?' said Marie, 'you look vair much like de leaf in von grand storm, all ovair wiz de shake!'

"'Well,' says I, 'I do feel as ef I wur about to col-lapse a flue, or bust my biler, for the fact of the marter is, Marie, they say your old daddy's a tiger, and ef I git caught here thar'll be suthin' broke—a buryin' in-stead of a weddin';—not that I'm the least mite skeered fur myself, but the old man might git hurt, and I should be fretted to do any sech a thing.'

"'Oh, *mon amie*, nevair be fear fur him, he is von great, strong as vat you call de gentleman cow?—von bull,—but, mon Dieu! what shall I do wiz you, sup-pose he come, eh? He vill cut you into bits all ovair!'

"'But, my angel,' ses I, 'he shant ketch me, fur I'll streak it like a fast boat, the moment I hear steam from his scape-pipe—the old man might as well try to catch a Massissippi *catty* with a thread line, as git his fingers on me.' I had no sooner said so, than *bang!* went the door below, and old Fecho, juicy as a melon, came feelin' his way up stairs, mutterin' like a small piece of fat thunder, and swarin' in French, orfully. I know'd thar warn't much time to spare, so I histed the winder and backed out. Jest as I was about to drop, Marie says to me—'Oh, *mon Dieu!* don't drop into de *vell!*' and instanter shut the winder. My *har* riz on eend in a moment—'*don't drop into the well!*' I'll tell you what, boys, a souse into the Massissippi in ice time warn't half as cold as her last warnin' made me. It was so etarnal dark that I couldn't begin to tell which side of the buildin' I wur on, and that wur an all important perticuler, fur it wur jest *three* stories high on one side, towards the Hollow, and it warn't only *one* on the side next the hill—in course, all the chances wur in favor of the *well* bein' on the low side. I'd gin all I had then to know which side was waitin' below fur me. I looked up, as I hung on, to see ef thar warn't a star shinin' somewhare, jest to give a hint of what *was* below, but they'd all put on thar night caps, and wouldn't be coaxed from under the kiver; then I'd look below, and listen, until I made sartin in my mind that I could hear the droppin' of water, somewhare about *fifty feet* below me! Old Fecho was a tearin' through the room, and a rippin' out French oaths, in an oncommon rapid manner, and declarin' that he knew some one had bin thar, fur he'd bin told so. Two or three times he appeared to be a rushin' for the winder, and the little gal would coax him back agin, and then he'd cuss de Yankee doodels, and grit his teeth most owdaciously. Well, ef I warn't in an oneasy situation all this time, then I'm more than human—my arms jest stretched out to about a yard and a half in length, and gin to cramp and git orful weak. I couldn't fur the life of me think on any prayer I'd ever heerd—at last, jest as one hand was givin' way its hold, I thort of a short one I used to say when I was a younker, and mutterin'—'Here I drop me down deep, I pray the Lord my bones to keep!' I sot my teeth together, drew a long breath, shut my eyes, and let go!—*whiz!—r-r-r-ip!—bang!* I went—as I supposed—about fifty feet; and didn't I holler, when I lit and rolled over, and the water soused all round me! 'Murder! oh, git me out, oh-o-o-o, mur*der!* The people came a rushin' out of their houses, with lights, and sich another jargon of questions as they showered at me—askin', all together, who'd bin a stabbin' me? what wur the marter? and who'd hit me? I opened my eyes to tell 'em I'd fell from the third story, and broke every bone in my body, when, on lookin' up, thar wur the old Frenchman and his darter, grinnin' out of the top winder, about *ten feet* above me! The fact wur, boys, I'd dropped out on the *hill side* of the house, and jumped down jest *four feet* from whar my toes reached,—I had lit on the edge of a water pail, and it flowed about me when I fell over! Arter old Fecho told them the joke, they pretty nigh busted a larfin' at me. I crawled off, arter firin' a volly at old Mounseer, of the hardest kind of cusses, and from that day to this I han't gone a courtin' in French Hollow!

THE SECOND ADVENT!

TOM BANGALL, THE ENGINEER, AND MILLERISM.

About the period fixed upon by Father Miller, for the general blowing up of the world, some of the engineers upon our western waters, who had been used to blowing up its inhabitants, became a little frightened at the prospect of having to encounter, in another world, the victims of steamboat disaster. Among these was Tom Bangall, the engineer of the Arkansas Thunder. Tom was a rearing, tearing, *bar* state scrouger—could chaw up any single specimen of the human race—any quantity of tobacco, and drink steam without flinching!—A collapsed flue had blown him once somewhere in the altitude of an Alpine height, but dropped him unharmed into the Arkansas, and he used to swear that after the steam tried to jerk him apart and found it couldn't do it, why, it just dropped the *subject*, as the stump speakers say, by dropping him into the "drink"—he therefore incontinently set water, hot or cold, at defiance. Tom was, withal, a generous, open-hearted, whole-souled fellow, and his cheering words to the emigrants on the boiler deck, and many a kind act to a suffering passenger, proved that beneath his rough exterior he had a heart open to gentle influences. As a further proof of this, Tom had a wife, a good wife, too, and what's more he tenderly loved her; but she in vain tried to cure him of drinking and swearing. Tom swore that he would swear, that a steamboat wouldn't work without some swearing, and if a fellar didn't drink he'd bust, and, therefore, it was necessary to take a *bust* now and then to keep out of danger. "There is no use," he would say, "in blowing off steam from your 'scape-pipe agin it, for it has to be *did!*"

One day on Tom's return home, he found Mrs. Mary Bangall weeping bitterly, and Tom became, instantly, correspondingly distressed.

"Why, Polly," inquired he, "what's the matter, gal?—what's hurt you?—is anythin' broke loose that can't be mended?—what the thunder makes you take on so?—Come, out with the cause, or I shall git a blubberin' too."

"Only look here, Tom," said Mary, "here's a whole account of how the world is going to be destroyed this April.—Every thing has been counted up by Father Miller, and the sum total's a general *burn!* Now, Tom, don't swear, nor drink any more or you won't be able to stand the fire no more than gunpowder!"

Tom indulged in a regular guffaw at her distress, and told her she was a fool to be frightened at that—it was all moonshine—humbug—smoke,—that Father Miller was an old granny, and it warn't possible—anyhow he warn't afraid of fire, so it might *fire away!*"

"But, Tom," continued Mary, "let me read to you the proof—it's irresistible, Tom,—the *times* and the *half times*, are so correctly added up that there can be no mistake, and if you don't make some preparation we will be separated for ever."

The idea of a separation from Mary troubled Tom, but full of incredulity he sat down to listen, more to please her, and find something in the adding up of the catastrophe that would upset it. Mary commenced reading, and Tom quietly listening, but as she read the awful evidences of a general conflagration, the signs of the times, the adding up of the times, the proof of their meaning, and the dreadful consequences of being unprepared—with ascension robes, Tom grew serious, and at length looked a little frightened. He didn't want Mary to see its effect upon him, and so assumed an over quantity of indifference, but it was useless for him to attempt hiding his feelings from her prying eyes—she saw Miller's doctrine was grinding a *hopper* of fear in Tom's heart, and felt glad to see its effect. When she ceased he remarked, with a half-frightened laugh, that Father Miller ought to be burnt for thus trying to frighten people, and, "as for them eastern fellars, they are half their life crazy any how!"

Having tried thus to whisper unconcern to his troubled spirit, Tom set out for the boat, with the firm resolve, if he caught a Millerite to save him from the threatened burning by drowning him, for disseminating any such fiery doctrines. When he got on board he told the captain what had transpired at home,—how his wife had got hold of a Miller document from a travelling disciple, and, as well as he could, rehearsed the awful contents which she had read to him. The captain, observing the effect they had produced on Tom, seriously answered that the matter looked squally, and he was afraid them documents were all too *true*.

"True!" shouted Tom, "why, you aint green enough to swallow any such yarn—its parfectly rediculous to talk about burnin' every thing up. I'd like to see old Miller set fire to the Massissippi!"

"Its no funny matter, Tom," replied the captain, "and if you keep going on this way you will find it so."

"Here, give us somethin' to drink!" shouted Tom to the bar-keeper, (he began to get terrified at the serious manner with which the captain treated Millerism) "come, Bill," said he, addressing the clerk, "let's take a drink."

The clerk, who was a wag, saw through the captain's joke in a minute and when he winked at him, refused to taste, adding as an apology that "on the eve of so awful an event as the destruction of the world, he couldn't daringly indulge as he formerly did, so he must excuse him."

"Well, go to h—ll, then," says Tom, half mad.

The captain sighed, and the clerk put his hand upon his heart, and turned his eyes upward, as if engaged in inward prayer for his wicked friend. Tom swallowed his glass, and bestowing a fierce look upon the pair remarked, that "they couldn't come any of them thar shines over him, he wasn't any of that *chicken breed!*"

"Poor fellow," muttered the captain.

"Alas! Thomas," chimed in the clerk.

Tom slammed the cabin door after him as he went out to descend below, swearing at the same time that all the rest of the world were turning damned fools as well as old Miller.

Steam was raised and the Thunder started. For a time Tom forgot the predicted advent, but every time he came up to the bar to get a drink, the serious look of the captain and the solemn phiz of the clerk, threw a cold chill over him, and made him savage with excitement. Every passenger appeared to be talking about Millerism, besides, a waggish friend of the captain's, a passenger on board, having been informed of the engineer's state of mind, passed himself off as a preacher of the doctrine, and talked learnedly on the prophecies whenever the engineer was nigh. It was comic to see the fierce expression of their victim's countenance, and how, in spite of himself, he would creep up to the circles where they were discussing the Second Advent, and listen with all ears to the rehearsal of its terrible certainty, then making for the bar, take another drink, and thrusting his hands deep into his pockets start down to the engine, with a scowl upon his swart countenance that would almost start a flue head from its fastenings.

"I'd quit this boat," said Tom to his assistant, "if it warn't so near 'the 25th of April,'—cuss me if I'd stay aboard another minit, fur captain and all hands are a set of cowardly *pukes!*"

"Why, what's the 25th of April got to do with your leavin', Tom?" inquired his partner.

"Nothin' particular, but if this confounded blow up or burn up should come off on that day, I wan't to be on the river—its safer; but if I should leave now I couldn't get on another boat by that time, and then I'd be in a *hot* fix."

Here was a tacit confession by Tom, that he thought there was danger, and that there might be some truth in old Miller's prediction. The fact of his fears was forthwith communicated to the captain and clerk by Tom's partner, and his sufferings became increased—he could hear no sounds but—*advent—Miller—blow-up—dreadful destruction!*—until his suspense became so horrible, that he wished for any termination so it would put an end to his dread. His partner ventured to increase his uneasiness by talking to him on the subject, but Tom threatened to brain him if he said anything about it in his presence—he remarked that "the noise of the engine was his only peace, and no frightened, lubberly sucker should disturb it by talking Millerism—if Miller was a goin' to burn the world, why, let him burn and be——(here, Tom for the first time checked an oath, and finished the sentence with) never mind, just let him *burn*, that's all."

Starting up to the bar, without looking to right or left, he presented a bottle, had it filled with liquor and retreated, resolved to go as little as possible near either captain or clerk, for their solemn looking faces were contagious—they looked disaster.

At length the 25th of April dawned, and with its advancing hours Tom got *tight*, that is to say, so near intoxicated that he could only move around with extreme difficulty—he knew what he was about, but very little more. Sundry mutterings which he gave voice to, now and then, proclaimed the spirit at work within, and it would say:—

"Burn, ha!—burn up, will it?—goin' to take a regular bust and blow itself out! Great world, this!—g-r-e-a-t world, and a nice little fire it *will* be!" Then, thinking of Mary, he would continue—"Poor Mary—what a shock it will be to her, but she's on the safe side, for she belongs to meetin';"—and then he would get wrathy—"Let the old world burn, and go to splintered lightnin'—who cares?—The captain and clerk's got on the safe side, too,—they're afraid of the fire, eh?" Then he would cautiously emerge from his place by the engine, and peep out upon the sky, to see if the work of destruction was about to commence, and then returning, take another pull at the whiskey, until, by his frequent libations, he not only got *blue*, but every thing he looked at was multiplying—he was surrounded by a duplicate set of machinery—even his fist, that he shook at the intruding cylinder and piston rod, became doubled before his eyes, and all assumed the color of a brimstone *blue!* Tom became convinced, in his own mind, that the first stage of the general convulsion had commenced!

"Hello!—back her!" shouted the captain, "give her a lick back!—starboard wheel, there!"

"It's all up, now," muttered Tom, "let's see you *lick* her back out of this scrape," and staggering towards the steam valves, to try the amount of water in the boilers, he fell sprawling; at that moment the boat struck the bank with a bang that shook every timber in her; the concussion, also, injured a conducting steam-pipe just enough to scald Tom's face and hands severely, without endangering his life. As the stream of hot vapour hit him, he rolled over, exclaiming:—

"Good God!—it's all up, now!" and soon became utterly insensible

Tom was picked up and carried into the Social Hall,

where restoratives were administered to recall him to consciousness, and remedies applied to heal his burns. All gathered in silence and anxiety around his pallet, watching for returning sensibility, the captain and clerk among the number, really grieved at the mishap, which they had no doubt was caused by their jest. While all breathlessly looked on, Tom gave manifestations of returning consciousness: of course, with sensibility returned feeling, and his burns appealed, most touchingly, to that sense. Twisting himself up, and drawing his breath through his teeth, he slowly remarked:—

"Jest as I thought—the d—l's got me, *s-l-i-c-k* enough, and I'm burnt already to a cinder!"

There was no resisting this—all hands burst into a roar of laughter. Tom couldn't open his eyes, but he could hear, and after they had done laughing, he quietly remarked:—

"These *imps* are mightily glad because they've got *me!*"

Here followed another roar, and when it subsided, the captain approached him, and called his name—

"Tom, old fellow," said he, you're safe!"

"What, *you* here, too, captain? I thought you had jined meetin' and saved your bacon.—So they've got you, too,—well, a fellar aint alone then."

Here the clerk spoke to him.

"What, you, too, Bill?—well, 'there's a party of us,' any how, but it's so confounded dark I can't see you, and its hotter than——(here he checked himself with a shudder, and added,) Yes, I'm certain we're *thar!*" sighing heavily, he murmured—"Poor Mary—Oh, my Mary."

By the efforts of the captain and clerk Tom was made to understand the true state of the case, and through their kindness and attention, was soon able to return to duty, and though he would after laugh at a jest about old Father Miller, yet he was never again known to drink whiskey. When irritated now, Tom always shuts his lips tight, and chokes down the rising oath. Mary is gratified with the change, although she wept at the severity of the means by which he was converted.

SETTLEMENT FUN.

BILL SAPPER'S LETTER TO HIS COUSIN.

LIBERTI, *Missury, May* 6*t*. 18 *forty* 5.

COUSIN JIM, tha aint nuthin' occurred wuth ritin' about in our settle*ment* fur a long spell, but about the beginnin' of last week, thur war a rumor sot afloat in town, which kept the wimen for two or three days in a continooal snigger, and it war half a day afore the men could find out the rights of the marter—sech anuther fease as all the gals got inter, war delightful to contemplate. The boys kept a askin' one anuther, what in the yearth wur the marter, that the gals kept a whisperin' and laffin' round town so—at last it cum out! and what do you think, Jim, *wur* the marter?—You couldn't guess in a week. It aint no common occurrence, and yet it's mighty natral. Little Jo Allen, the shoemaker, had an addition to his family, amountin' to jest *three babbys*—one *boy* and *two* gals! His wife is a leetle creatur', but I reckon she's "some" in countin' the census, and sech anuther excitement as her little brood of pretty babbys has kicked up among the wimen, is perfectly inticin' to bachelors. When the interestin' marter war furst noised about, the wimen wouldn't believe it, but to know the rights of it tha put on thur bonnets and poured down to see little Mrs. Allen, in a parfect stream of curiosity; and, sure enough, thar tha wur, three raal peert lookin' children, all jest alike. Bein' an acquaintance of Jo's he tuck me in to see his family, and it wur raaly an interestin' sight to see the little creaturs. Thar tha wur, with thur tiny faces aside each other, hevin on the prettiest caps,—all made and fixed by the young wimen, as a present to the mother,—and then thur infantile lips jest openin', like so many rose buds poutin', while thur bits of hands, transparent as sparmacity, wur a curtin' about and pushin', all doubled up, agin thur little noses, and thur mother all the time lookin' at 'em so peert and pleased, jest as ef she war feelin' in her own mind tha war hard to beat—addid to which, thar stood thur *daddy*, contemplatin', with a glow of parentil feelin', the whole unanimous pictur! It aint in me, Jim, to fully describe the univarsel merits of sech a scene, and I guess it couldn't receive raal jestis from any man's pen, 'cept he'd ben the father of *twins* at least.

"Gracious me," sed Mrs. Sutton, a very literary womin, who allays talks history on extra occasions, "ef that little Mrs. Allen aint ekill to the mother of the *Grashi!*"

She looked at little Jo, the daddy, fur a spell, and tuk to admirin' him so that she could scacely keep her hands off on him—*she* hadn't no babbys, poor womin!

"Ah, Mister Allen," ses she, "you are suthin' like a husbind—you're detarmin'd to descend a name down to your *ancesters!*"

I raaly believe she'd a kissed him ef thur hadn't ben so many wimen thar. The father of the babbys wur mitely tickled at furst, 'cause all the wimen wur a praisin' him, but arter a spell he gin to look skary, for go whar he would he found some wimen tryin' to git a look at him—tha jest besieged his shop winder, *all* the time, and kept peepin' in, and lookin' at him, and askin' his age, and whar he cum from? At last sum of the gals got so curious tha asked him whar he *did* cum from, *any how*, and as soon as he sed India*nee*, Dick Mason becum one of the popularest young men in the settle*ment*, among the wimen, jest 'cause he war from the same state.

Things went on this way fur a spell, till at last tha heerd of 'em in the country, and the wimen all about found some excuse to come to town to git store goods, jest a purpose to see the babbys and thur parents. The little daddy war wusser plagued now, and they starr'd at him so that he couldn't work—the fact wur his mind war gittin' troubled, and some of the wimen noticed the skary look he had out of his eyes, and kept a wonderin' what it meant. One mornin' it war noticed by some of the gals that his shop warn't open'd, so tha got inquirin' about him, and arter a sarch he cum up missin' —well, I'm of the opinion thar wur an excitement in town then, fully ekill to the president's election. Every womin started her husbind out arter Jo, with orders not to cum back without him, and sech a scourin' as tha gin the country round would a caught anythin' human—it *did* ketch Jo—on his road to *Texas!* When tha got him back in the town agin, a committee of married men held a secret talk with him, to larn what the marter wur, that he wanted to clear out, and Jo told 'em that the wimen kept a starin' at him so he couldn't work, and ef he war kept from his bisness, and his family continooed to increase *three* at a time, he'd git so cussed poor he'd starve, and tharfore he knew it 'ud be better to clar out, for the wimen would be sure to take good care of his wife and the babbys.

Old Dr. Wilkins wur appinted by the men to wait on a meetin' of the wimen, and inform them of the fact, that tha wur annoyin' the father of the three babbys, and had amost driven him out'n the settle*ment*. The Doctor, accordin' to appintment, informed the wimen, and arter he had retired tha went into committee of the whole, upon the marter, and appinted three of thur number to report at a meetin', on the next evenin', a set of resolutions tellin' what tha'd do in the premises, and governin' female action in the partickler case of Jo Allen, his little wife, and three beautiful healthy babbys.

When the hour of meetin' had arriv, Mrs. Sutton's parlors wur crowded with the wimen of the settle*ment*, and arter appinten Widder Dent to the *cheer* tha reported the committee on resolves reddy, and Mrs. Sutton bein' the head of the committee she sot to work and read the followin' drawn up paper :—

Whereas, It has ben sed by the wise Solomon of old that the world must be peopled, tharfore, we hold it to be the inviolate duty of every man to git married, and, moreover, rear up citizens and future mothers to our glorious republick ; and,

Whereas, It is gratifyin' to human natur', the world in gineral, Missury at large, and Liberty in partickler, that this settle*ment* has set an example to the *ancesters* of future time, which will not only make the wimen of this enlightened state a pattern for thur children, but a envy to the royal wimen of Europe, not forgettin' the proud mother of the Lions of Ingland, but will elevate and place in and among the furst families, fur ever hereafter, the mother that has shed such lustre upon the sex in gineral; and

Whereas, It is the melancholy lot of some to be deprived of doin' thar duty in the great cause of human natur', because the young men is back'ard about speakin' out, it is time that some measures be taken *inimical* to our general prosperity, and encouragin' to the risin' generation of young fellars round town; tharfore,

Resolved, That, as married wimen, our sympathies, like the heavin' of natur's bosom, yearns with admiration and respect fur that little womin, Mrs. Allen, and as we see her three dear little babbys, reclinin' upon thur mother's female maternal bosom, our beatin' hearts with one accord wish we could say ditto.

Resolved, That in the case of Mrs. Allen we see an illustrious example of the intarnal and extarnal progress of that spreadin' race, the Angel Saxons; and time will come when the mothers of the west will plant thar glorious shoots from one pinnacle of the Rocky Mountains to the tother, and until thar cry of *liberti* will be hollered from one pint to the next in a continooal *skreech!*

Resolved, That Mister Joseph Allen, the father of these three dear little babbys, shall receive a monument at his *deth*, and while he is livin', the wimen shall ony visit his shop once a week to look at him, 'cept the married wimen, who shall be permitted to see him twice a week and no offener, pervided and exceptin' tha want to git measured fur a par of shoes.

Resolved, Mister Joseph Allen shall hev the custom

of the whole settle*ment*, for he is a glorious livin' example of a dotin' husbind.

Arter these resolutions had ben unanimously passed, Mrs. Sutton addressed the meetin', in a stream of elegance, wharin she proved, clar as a whistle, that a family war the furst consideration fur a settler in a new country and town lots the arter question. "She acknowledged the corn," she sed, "that it war soothin' to look offen at thur neighbor Allen, but his peace of mind war the property of his family, and she hoped the ladies wouldn't disturb it, 'cause the loss of sech a husbind, would be a sufferin' calamity to the settle*ment*."

The meetin' adjourned, and Jo went back to work, singin' and whistlin' as happy as usual, and ever sence he's had a parfect shower of work, for the gals all round the country keep goin' to him to git measured, tha say he *desarves* to be incouraged.

Your furst Cousin,

BILL SARPER.

"DOING" A LANDLORD.

A STORY OF SHAPE AND TALENT.

TOM C. H——, Esq., a genius, whose ideas of life were on such a magnificent scale that they outran his interest, capital and all, was seated upon the porch of a fashionable hotel, in a large eastern *village*, one bright Monday morning, cogitating how, in the nature of things, it was possible for him to compass a dinner. The long score, unpaid, which stood recorded on the books within, precluded the idea of getting one there without the *tin*, and numerous searches through sundry pockets about his person were unrewarded by a single shiner. The case was desperate, but great minds are always equal to great emergencies, and Tom's was of that order. His coat had been renovated by a scourer, for whom he had written a love letter, his hat had been ironed by a good-natured hatter, who had enjoyed his custom in better days, a new coat of japan varnish had been lavished upon his cane, his dicky was passable, and no gentleman would think of examining the *extremities* of his covering, or pry into the *shifts* he had been put to for a *shirt*. Tom thought himself passable, and he resolved to pass off for a dinner, if possible. A stranger lolling easily on a settee near him looked vulnerable, and Tom, approaching him in a very bland and friendly manner, remarked :—

"Excuse me, sir, but you look so like an old friend of mine, J. B——, who has resided for years in the south, that I can't help addressing you."

"I am from the south, sir," answered the stranger, courteously, "but not the person you speak of—know him, however, and am pleased to encounter a friend of his."

"That's it," said Tom to himself, "got him as easy as rolling off a log!"

An animated conversation ensued, which ended by Tom being asked to dine, and when the gong proclaimed the table spread, in walked the stranger and Tom, arm-in-arm, large as life and twice as natural. He called the waiters with an air of ease, passed the stranger's wine with friendly freedom, laughed musically, jested with spirit, wiped his mouth with grace, and, in short, completely captivated the southerner. During the period of Tom's luxuriating, he was observed by the landlord, who, indignant, sent a servant to order him from the table. Tom had "come it" over him for so many odd dinners, without a shadow of prospect for pay, that he would stand it no longer. The servant approached, whispered in his ear, and stood off to give him room to *move.* Tom clutched the wine bottle, with the intention of hurling it at his head, but altered his purpose, and poured out another glass, drank it off, looked daggers at the servant, and in a moment more smiled confidence upon his friend.

"Would you believe it," said Tom, to the southerner, "that since my absence from the city for a few days past, a rival house of our *shipping firm* has whispered the possibility of our failure, and this rascally landlord, having heard the calumny, has insulted me here at table by sending a servant to demand the trifling sum I owe him."

The southerner was burning with indignation.

"It is too humiliating;" added Tom, "not dreaming of such an outrage, I am entirely unprovided at the moment."

"Here, my dear fellow," promptly proffered his friend, "here is my pocket-book, make use of it without hesitation."

"You're very kind," said Tom, "very, I will but borrow this thousand dollar bill for a moment—I know the rascal can't change it!"

With an air of offended dignity, Tom approached the office of the hotel, the landlord, frowning with anger, stood at the desk, the offended "diner out," put his hand to his eyes, as if hiding deep emotion, and then addressing the landlord in a grief-stricken voice, he said:

"I never areamed of such an insult from *you*, sir, at such a time, too, just as my uncle in the south has expired,—and his agent with me to deliver up the portion bequeathed to me—it is—it—*sir*, I cannot express in language my feelings. Take out of that the paltry sum I owe you,"—throwing down the thousand dollar bill,—"and henceforth I never will enter your door. Just at a time too," he further added, "when I had intended to make your house my home, and endeavor to make some return for your forbearance. It is too much—my feelings are lacerated," and here he became almost overpowered by emotion.

The strip of crape around his hat—put there to hide the greasy band—the thousand dollar bill, and the renovated coat, which looked like new on the possessor of such a sum, all assured the landlord that he had been *hasty*. He, therefore, denied the indignity, straight, said that it was an impertinence of his servant, who had *twice* before offended his best guests by his insolence, and assured Tom that he would discharge the fellow forthwith—pushed back to him the thousand dollar bill, and begged he would forget the circumstance—indeed, he felt shocked that such an outrage had been perpetrated upon his *oldest* friend and customer. These warm expressions mollified Tom's wrath, and folding up his bill he walked back, resumed his seat, returned the bill to the southerner, merely remarking he had "brought the landlord to his feelings," and cheerfully sipped a *little* iced champagne. As he left the table arm-in-arm with his freind, the landlord approached, bowing, and begged to know where he shculd send for his trunk, as No. 24, a fine airy room, which would suit him to a charm, was at present empty. Tom said he would send the baggage up, and after lighting a choice Havana, strolled out with an air aristocratic.

In good time, the trunk arrived--a rude one, but *very heavy*. The landlord winked as the servant bent beneath its weight, and remarked, as *he* paid the porterage, that a large quantity of *bullion* was generally rather heavy. Tom was in clover—the thousand dollar bill got whispered about, and one of his creditors, a fashionable tailor, insisted on *trusting* him for another suit; he yielded, after much persuasion, and it was astonishing how everything altered with Tom's appearance. His note was good for any small sum now, and it was a pleasure to make his acquaintance.

In the course of about *six* months the landlord thought he would just hint to Tom that a small check would be agreeable, as they were hard pushed. The hint was given, and he received a *check*—anything but a cash one, though. Tom very coolly informed him that the agent who had raised his hopes was a rascally impostor.

"But the thousand dollar bill, Mr. H.?" said the landlord, inquiringly.

"Was handed to me, by the rogue, to keep up appearances," coolly responded Tom.

"I shall seize your baggage, sir!" cried the enraged host.

"I can't help it, my dear fellow," said Tom; "you know if I had a 'pocket full of *rocks*,' you should share them, for I like you, vastly—I do—cuss me if I don't; so keep cool, and keep the baggage until I make a draw and raise the little sum."

The trunk *was* seized, and so roughly that it burst

open, when the landlord discovered that if Tom had no *pocket* full of *rocks*, it was because he had stowed them all in his *trunk*, and that accounted very naturally for its being so heavy!

WHO IS SIR GEORGE SIMPSON?

AN EXTRAORDINARY CIRCUMSTANCE ABOUT HIM.

An esteemed friend of ours, who now, heaven rest his spirit, sleeps in the tomb, had a curious method of relating a story; and if his hearer was of an impatient nature, it would be sorely tried before he heard the conclusion of any yarn the "Consul" might start to favor him with. On one occasion, some months since, he seated himself at my elbow, while I was busily perusing a piece of news in which Sir George Simpson's name appeared, and taking the knight's cognomen for a text, he insisted on relating to me an extraordinary circumstance, which drew forth a correspondingly extraordinary remark from the said Sir George. With a pencil, unperceived by the relater, I stenographed his story, nearly word for word, and as it is replete with interest, I do not feel justified in withholding it at the present time from the public; so, here it is:—

"I'll tell you an *extraordinary* circumstance about George Simpson," said the "Consul." "You see, when I was at my brother's, on Staten Island, some years since—at his country seat, living with his family—(my brother Bill, it was)—there was some six children, and I lived at home there—the oldest not more than fourteen, and I used to take him out hunting with me;—the young rascal was a good shot, too! You see I was there at that time on my oars, doing nothing, and had plenty of time to spare, which I used to fill up by fishing and hunting, sometimes for days together—pretty poor luck at that, often, but I didn't care, as time wasn't valuable. Well, you see, my brother Bill used to invite some of the people in the neighborhood to dinner, and often there were distinguished visiters on the island—it's a first rate place in summer—and Bill had every thing nice on his table; he took some trouble to keep it fine, and he had a reputation for being a good liver. You could see he liked good things by his appearance, for he was corpulent. Well, you see, Sir George Simpson happened to be invited to dine—Sir George, the Scotchman, old fellow—belonging to the Hudson Bay Fur Company; Scotch as the devil!—old tory at that; he has travelled all over the north-western territory, and Oregon, and clear up to Behring's Strait; knows the worth of a wild-cat skin in any market in the world, old Sir George does—a cursed old Jew, too! Well, as we were all seated at the table—I on my brother Bill's right, and Sir George on his left—(Sir George was dressed in check pants and a snuff-colored coat, looking as pompous as the red lion of England, although he was only a Scotch clerk of the Fur Company)—just as Bill's oldest boy asked for something at table, and I was helphim to a bit of veal kidney—the young rascal was fond of kidney, and would have it when it was on the table—says Sir George, says he—and my brother Bill, who was just turning up his plate at the time, stopped and laid down his fork, and I turned round to hear what he had to say—(the old fellow always spoke slow, with considerable Scotch accent, and every body wanted to hear—it's the most extraordinary circumstance or remark, whichever you please, as I said, that ever I heard)—says Sir George, says he, "*I shouldn't wonder if we have to fight about Oregon yet!*"

LETTERS FROM A BABY.

BY A FORWARD CHILD.

St. Louis has obtained the reputation of being a dangerous climate for infants, and the bills of mortality, as they have from time to time exhibited an alarming number of deaths among children, have called forth learned disquisitions from the "medicine men," and some new views from those who are without the pale of regular practice. All seemed to agree that the mortality every summer was alarming, but no two united in assigning the same cause for the fatal result. After listening patiently to both sides, I sought information from the suffering party, and their opinion may be gathered from the complaints of their correspondent *Bub*. He says:

Dear Sir:—Of late I perceive the public are making some stir about us babies; may heaven vouchsafe healthy children to our defenders. I have a string of sorrows to relate myself, and my poor bowels cry out for protection; you must therefore permit me to say a few words. My Ma is what you would call a fashionable woman, and although she loves her baby, yet she says it is not fashionable for mammas in the southern states to nurse their own babies; I am, consequently, turned over to the care of nigger Molly, and Lord preserve me, such nursing as I get would kill a young *Indian.* I am fed with every thing, from a green apple to a chunk of fat pickled pork, and the sufferings which I undergo therefrom, would crack a sucking bottle, or rend a diaper in tatters. After feeding me into sickness, they set a doctor at me, who physics me into a state of quiet insensibility, and they then say, "bess its ittle bessed heart it's ditten better, it is." I get a little peace until I get strong enough to cry out, and then nigger Molly stuffs me to keep me quiet, and I go through another spell. I see our dog Flora watching her pups, and if any person goes near them she is almost ready to tear them to pieces; I wish my Ma was as careful of me. I see a poor woman opposite kissing her baby, and I envy that child; nobody kisses me but black Molly, and she does it to smother my cries of suffering. I don't know what kills other babies, but this treatment will soon finish me BUB.

NO. II.—BUB IN PERIL.

How are you?—You have published my letter, and I am glad to see that nigger Molly cannot smother my cry to the public—if I don't give her *scissors*, it will be because she smothers me outright. You must know Molly keeps two bottles filled with liquid, one of which she administers to me, and the other to herself, and they both have about the same effect, only hers smells worst. Hers she calls *whiskey*, mine *cordial.* The other morning Molly set me down on the floor, beside a pan of water, and commenced taking comfort from her bottle, and I, feeling feverish, commenced comforting myself by dabbling in the pan until I was all wet; Molly perceiving this picked me up to *slap* me, but *her* cordial floored her. I should have been glad of this, only she nearly killed me in her fall, and because I screamed, as any baby would do, she clapped her black lips to mine, smelling horribly as they were of whiskey, and kept in my breath until I was as black in the face as herself. I yelled at this double outrage, and she silenced me by pouring a double dose of *cordial* down my throat, which threw me into a state of insensibility, from which I awoke almost dead. My mother asked to see me, and when she heard me moaning, she said "the ittle bessed dear is suffering wis its too-sys." I aint suffering with my teeth—I'm suffering with nigger Moll's nursing.

BUB.

NO. III.—BUB RESCUED.

Hello, boys:—Flourish trumpets! merrily beat your drums—I'm a saved *sucker!* A day of hope and promise has shed its light upon my infantile head, and bright visions of a pair of small breeches to be worn by me, float airily round my head—they appear plain and palpable in the vista of the future—buttons, pockets, suspenders and all—*vive la pantalons!* The other morning my Pa drew forth the copies of the Reveille from his book case, and commenced reading them for Ma's amusement. Suddenly he cast his eye on my letters, and straight he commenced them—he laughed, and then Ma laughed, and then I crowed. By and by, as he proceeded, Ma began to look angry; she cast a glance at me, and then her conscience smote her—I was wasted to a shadow—on went Pa with the letters; Ma wept, I crowed, and nigger Molly gave me a *pinch*—a yell followed and the clouds burst!

"Give me that child, you hateful jade, you; how dare you hurt it?" cried Ma.

"Please God, I didn't do nuffin ob de sort, missus; I'd do any thin else, missus, dan hurt de baby," answered Moll.

"Get out of my sight, you hussy!" cried my enraged mamma; "you have nearly killed de bessed ittle pet—mamma's dear, bess its heart—get out of my sight; if ever you touch it again, I'll punish you severely."

Molly fled, Pa chuckled to himself, and I crowed again—I tried to hurrah! How shall I describe the change which stole over me, body and spirit, as, nestling in my mother's sweet bosom and receiving her fond caress, I was permitted abundantly to drink at "Nature's *pure* fount, which, at my cry, sent forth a pearly stream to cherish my enamelled veins." A sweet sleep visited my pillow again, and the fond endearments which waited on my waking moments were life and joy to me. My Ma, now, is rapidly improving in health—I, of course, will grow fat; and just wait until I'm able to wear *them* breeches and beat a small *drum*, if I don't visit the Reveille office and give you the serenade of "Oh, be joyful," until your petrified stump will execute a double shuffle, then say my name aint BUB.

NO. IV.—BUB FLOURISHING.

Hello, Drummers: — Whoop! hey! cock-a-doodle-doo-o-o! If I aint some by this time I wouldn't say so! You remember what a sickly state I was in when I commenced telling you my grievances? — how my complaints wrought improvement and rescued me from nigger Molly? Well, ever since then, it's a surprise to learn the way my body has spread—I'm a small *Lambert*, and have got *six teeth*. Aint I some? Talk of your Missouriums!—only look at me! Well, between you and me, I didn't cut them teeth for nothing; I find a fellow don't get knowledge without paying for it; I suffered in teething, but I learned some. Women who pay no attention to their babies, envy me my *fat*—I'm a kind of living rebuke to them, and, for a year old, I'm rather a *heavy* rebuke. They every now and then say: "Why, bless me, Mrs. T——, you'll kill yourself nursing that big fat child." The answer they get, generally, is, "Well, *it* will get killed if I *don't!*" That's the way to tell it!—bravo, Ma! "Well, but, Mrs. T——, why don't you let Molly relieve you of such a load?" Ma answers, "It's because Molly nearly *relieved* me of him altogether—he would have died from her nursing." That's a fact!—hit 'em again, Ma. "*My* children," says Mrs. Nevernurse, "get along very well without me." "Yes," answered Ma, again, "you have only *two* living out of *six*." That was a wiper!—how she twisted her face at it! I think I'm safe enough, but my peace is sadly troubled with fear when I hear some of these old women giving Ma advice. It would do you good to see old Molly look at me, now and then, saying, with her big eyes, "Well, bress de Lord, I'm clar ob dat brat, but I should jis like to hab him for a a week, I'd take de sassy look out ob his face." I'd like to try my six new teeth on her black hide.

You shall have that serenade, Drummers, and no mistake. BUB.

NO. V.—BUB AGAIN IN DANGER.

Gents:—How d'ye do? I've just had a good long pull at the titty, and have got on a clean warm diaper; and feeling pretty comfortable, I think I'll give you another small epistle. I'm going to get into trouble—I feel it in my bones. My Ma has quarreled with her old physician, and has employed a new one, young Dr. Pliant—between you and me, I think they should have named him *Verdant*. This new doctor wants to please, so anything the women propose is exactly right. "Don't you think, Doctor," says one, "that Mrs. T—— will destroy her health, nursing that fat child?" "Certainly, maam, most unquestionably, Mrs. Helpalong; the strength of the mother being inadequate to the sufficient indevelopment of the ponderous system of meat-gather-upon-its-bones-ativeness of the infant, it consequently follows that the thin-down-to-a-light-altitudity of the fill-up-and-get-strong-ative powers of the mother naturally must result." "I thought so, Doctor," says Mrs. Helpalong, and this clear-as-mud evidence against my comfort is reiterated to my mother. "Do you really think, Dr. P., that I am endangering my health?" "That depends upon how you feel," says the doctor. "Why," says Ma, "I feel as well as ever I did in my life." "Your system, then," says the doctor, "is what we call in the south *sui generis*—that is, you can stand nursing, and, consequently, the babe having a tendency to the natural milk which surreptitiously flows, I might say, from the secretive portion of the female *os frontis* of the breast, it must follow, as a result from these multifarious and indigenous effects, that no danger can ensue from your nursing." I'm safe as long as my mother keeps in good health; but Lord bless me, should she get ill, I'm a gone *sucker*—this new physician would dose her and me into kingdom come in about a week. I heard quite a discussion about his merits yesterday. Mrs. Enquiry says that he used to be a fiddler about two years ago, but Mrs. Helpalong says it is no such thing—that he always was a gentleman, and taught school before he took up the profession —that he studied regularly a whole season, and took his diploma in the spring;—she sticks to that, Mrs. Helpalong does, and I guess she is about right. Aint my case critical?

BUB.

NO. VI.—BUB'S RECEPTION OF A SILVER PAP SPOON.

I'm here again:—Important events having transpired since I last wrote to you, it has been deemed proper to send a synopsis of them to you for publication, in order that the world in general may know western babies are *some*, and when well nursed a good deal *more* than some. A most gratifying reformation has been effected in certain circles by my letters, and, indeed, wherever they have been read, nigger nurses, paregoric, sucking-bottles, coarse diapers, and sundry other abuses have entirely disappeared. The effect has been a corresponding improvement in babies, generally, and your correspondent in particular, who is now admitted to be a *whapping* child for a small family.

On last Christmas, a number of our parents having met together to celebrate the day, all of us youngsters were put into the nursery together, and the clatter of discussion which followed would have thrown a peevish nurse into hysterics. Charley Wilgus proposed that a meeting should be held upon the spot, and a *silver pap spoon* voted to me for my able letters in defence of infantile rights. Asa Keemle seconded the motion, and it was unanimously carried. Charley Wilgus was thereupon chosen chairman, and Asa Keemle, secretary. The president mounted a pillow, and called the meeting to order by ringing the bells on his coral. On motion, a committee was then appointed to draft resolutions expressive of the sense of the meeting, and the following boys, having cut their eye-teeth, were selected to draft said resolutions:

Augustus Vinton, Edward Shade, John Charless, Christopher Wigery, John Dalrymple and Wallace Finney.

The committee having retired, Colton A. Presbury, Jr., offered the following resolution, which he prefaced by some very pertinent remarks:

Resolved, That *cutting* teeth is a *sharp* operation, and should therefore, be deferred until maturity.

Presbury G. A. Colton, a little fellow who had just cut his first "double," opposed this resolution, on the ground of its interfering with "future prospects,"—he went in for teeth now, and the cutting to come being left an open question. The resolution was rejected.

Rucker Smith now rose to address the meeting, when some objection was made to him because he sucked milk from a bottle; it was, however, concluded that he might address the chair if his diaper was pinned tight; on examination he was permitted to proceed. He commenced describing the horrors of a *cold bath*, and was interrupted by the president, who informed him that the subject of *water* came more particularly under the head of *streams*, and could not then be entertained by the meeting. He then proceeded to describe the delights of a *sucking-bottle*, and was *cried* down by the unanimous voice of the meeting. Some one now commenced a speech against *paregoric*, whereupon the assembly, speaker and all, went immediately to *sleep!*

They were aroused from their slumber by the return of the committee, which, through their chairman, Augustus Vinton, reported the following resolutions:

Resolved, That babies are, and of right ought to be, natural-born *suckers*.

Resolved, That the introduction of negro nurses among white babies was a *dark* era in infantile history.

Resolved, That all artificial efforts, in regard to babies, are no go, and that the old fashion defies the ingenuity of Yankee*dom* to improve on it.

Resolved, That "being born with a silver spoon in your mouth" is a good thing, but an unlimited chance at the *titty* is a better.

Resolved, That all anti-nursing mothers are undeserving of lively husbands.

Resolved, That we look with feelings of compassion upon those who have *adopted* children.

Resolved, That *Bub* deserves a *silver pap spoon*, and shall have one.

These resolutions having been unanimously adopted by the meeting, it was—

On motion of O. M. Ridgely, seconded by Edward Shade, adjourned. A general call was now made for refreshments, which anxious mothers promptly supplied.

Yours, Bub.

SETH TINDER'S FIRST COURTSHIP

HOW HIS FLAME WAS QUENCHED!

You knew Seth Tinder,—No?—"git eout!"—you did know Seth, every body knew him, and they couldn't help it, for Seth would know every body. He was, perhaps, the "cutest critter," in some things, that ever calculated the success of a notion expedition, and he was among the first of his genus that ever strayed, on such an expedition, as far west as St. Louis. If you really didn't know Seth, it is time your ignorance was enlightened.

Seth was remarkably cute at driving a bargain—that was an innate propensity; Seth was inquisitive, and frequently looked into hall doors, and peeped into kitchen windows—that was Yankee human nature; Seth winked at the girls—that was an acquired habit; he resolved to possess one—that was a *calculation*. Now, this winking at the girls, when performed by a handsome individual, is looked upon as a matter of course; but Seth was so notoriously ugly, that his wink was an outrage, and his overtures of love, perfect atrocities. His short, bow-legged figure was thatched with the most obstinate bunch of carroty hair that ever bid defiance to bear's oil, and the windows of his mind as the eyes are poetically styled, appeared looking intently at the tip of his nose, as if apprehensive that, ere long, it would burst into a blaze. A kind of half-burnt-prairie garnished his chin, which would have made a very *warm* looking *goatee*, if Seth could have transplanted it all to one spot; but there lay the difficulty, for though cute at driving a bargain, he could make none with nature—she made him ugly without his consent, and wouldn't agree to any alteration. Seth, nevertheless, would wink at the girls.

His first tender effort was made upon the heart of a German butcher's fair, fat, rosy daughter, whose round cheeks and well-fed form was, to his eye, the very perfection of female beauty. No artificial making up about her—no exterior padding, it was all done naturally, on the inside. As she luxuriated upon the door steps of an evening, Seth would linger near, wink, and grin all sorts of affection, but, like all bashful swains, hesitated about coming to close quarters. He had imbibed the erroneous opinion, that all true courting must be done clandestinely; but all his hints to draw his inamorata into a secret treaty, was a failure. At length, he ventured in a desperate manner up to the door step, and whispered hurriedly:—

"Look out—comin' to set up with you to-night—round the back way—over the fence—be a-waitin'!"

"You'd petter pe ketch'd," was the fair one's rejoinder, accompanied by a malicious laugh, which Seth interpreted as an approving one.

The darkness of the night favored Seth's clandestine opinions and practice--it was just the thing for a noc-

"They found their trusty sentry baulking all Seth's efforts to retreat over the fence, and keeping him 'a waitin'!"—*Page* 179.

turnal visit; therefore, agreeable to notice, he made his appearance at the fence, round the back way. Leaning over the barrier, he ventured to sound a cautious "hist," which was immediately answered by a low "wou-ugh." That must be Dutch for "come," reasoned Seth, and straight he mounted the fence; but politician never took an uneasier seat on the same line of division than he *enjoyed* on the present occasion, for, no sooner had one pedal extremity reached the other side and placed him fairly astride, than a remarkably savage dog seized the intruding member, with a fierce "wou-ugh-ugh-ugh-u."

"Git eout, you blasted critter!" shouted Seth.

"Wou-ugh-ugh!" roared the dog.

A struggle ensued, in which Seth, unfortunately, fell on the wrong side, right into the jaws of his antagonist. The attitude in which he reached terra firma, offered the dog a change of grip, and, like a skilful sentinel, he seized the advantage and Seth's seat of honor at the same time. Our hero sprang nearly erect, with a howl more like his antagonist than any human noise, and a desperate struggle, mingled with strange cries, aroused the dozing butcher from his pipe, and the fair cause of the disturbance from her knitting.

"Sum tam rascal's after der sausages in der smoke haus!" was the butcher's first exclamation; the rosy daughter smiled assent, and "arm and out," was the work of an instant. They found their trusty sentry baulking all Seth's efforts to retreat over the fence, and keeping him "*a-waitin'*" when he would have given worlds to leave. The reinforcement made at him with whip and broomstick, and this terrible odds aroused him to superhuman exertions;—with a "muzzler" he floored the Dutchman and his pipe, charged on the flinty-hearted daughter, captured her broomstick, beat a parley with it on the dog's head, and retreated over the fence with "flying colors"—*sticking through a rent of his inexpressibles.*

THE DEATH STRUGGLE;

OR, THE WAY SMITH DID UP JONES.

You all knew Smith—every body knew Smith, and Smith was known by every body—consequently, Smith was considered somebody. A body is supposed to contain a soul; Smith's body not only contained a soul, but certain parts of Smith's body made and mended other men's *soles.* Smith was enterprising, industrious, and won thereby the sole control of the boot and shoe business of the flourishing town of Kipp. Smith was a thriving man, a persevering man; Smith was, in fact, a strip of upper-leather. Just about the time of his greatest success, when the tide of fortune appeared to bear upon its surface a perfect skin of Smith's manufactured high-lows, and earth shook beneath the tread of his patent cork soles, along came *Jones.* Strange freak of fate! Jones was an adventurer,—a desperate adventurer,—a fellow who had made *soles* his study and upper leather his dream; he was a Napoleon in his business, and could slash calf-skin into a killing shape for pedal extremities;—in short, he was boot No. 1, both in the manufacture and sale of the article. In Jones' wanderings along the streets of Kipp, his eye fell upon the broad sign of "*Smith, Fashionable Boot and Shoe Maker.*" There was something prosperous and aristocratic about it, but, at the "Fashionable," Jones turned up his nose.

"Ox-hide fashion," says Jones, "Good common article, but won't sell alongside of a prime one. I'll drive that fellow, Smith, out of Kipp town—have it all to myself—do a smashing business—re-sole the town—become upper-leather in the community—president of town council—die mayor of the borough, and have all my own manufactured shoes walking at my funeral.—Lofty thought," added Jones.

In a very short time, upon the principal street in Kipp, in sight of Smith's, out swung a large *flag*, with the name of "Jones, importer, manufacturer, and patent leather boot and shoe *artiste.*" Smith stared, the flag fluttered, and Jones chuckled. Customers began to patronise Jones, and the flag seemed saucily to triumph, as it floated upon the breeze blowing towards Smith's door. Smith was a man of energy, though, and out came his new "patent gaiter boot;" the tide turned and Smith was again in the ascendant. Now began a leather war —Jones up and Smith down, Smith up again and Jones down, as each rival, alternately, brought out something new. At length, one bright morning, the inhabitants of Kipp, who had taken sides in the contest, were astounded by the appearance of the front of Smith's store—it was one entire sign, from the pavement to the roof. Jones looked blue, the flag fluttered like a tattered rag. Smith rose in importance—his friends felt proud of him —it was a Kipp triumph over foreign capital—the Jones party wavered!—not so Jones; his great mind had conceived a stupendous overthrow for Smith, and ere admiration for his rival had settled into sure success, it was diverted to himself. An immense flag, *of stone*, with his name in large letters, was scientifically planted right in the centre of Jones' pavement.

The town now became feverish with excitement, and it was rumored that the town council intended to consider the matter—the "signs of the times" grew alarming.

Glorious Smith!—Smith for ever!—unyielding to the last! In this emergency, when the horizon seemed heavy with defeat, when a vast stone seemed to press his fortunes into the earth, Smith arose, Phœnix like, "from a boot," and gave assurance to the world that he was no common leather. Rapid as the thought which conceived the idea, he had a vast boot constructed, placed upon a post in front of his door, and with a sample of his manufacture in each hand, he mounted into it, to exhibit to the passers by not only a spectacle of indomitable energy, but un-*flag*-ging perseverance.

"What do you think of Smith now?" said the adherents of the "big boot,"—"bravo, Smith!" shouted the Kippites. Here was a climax to which ingenuity could discover no parallel, it was indeed the *ne plus ultra*.

Jones put his hands behind his coat-tails, and looked up street at the big boot and its tenant, then at the stone flag beneath his feet, and his countenance settled into a calm and desperate determination. "I'll do it!" exclaimed he. The expression was caught up by his friends, wafted through the town, and whispered in each dwelling, until the excitement and expectation grew painful. Everybody was aching to see what Jones *would do*.

Jones cut out a capacious pair of boots, set his workmen at them, had them finished, sent every living soul away from his shop at early candle-light, closed it up, and all remained a mystery for the remainder of the night. Morning broke—astonishment and horror!—terrible Jones!—triumphing in death! He had drawn on the immense boots, fastened them by suspenders across his shoulders, and then suspended himself from the flag-staff right over the *flag-stone.* Beneath him fluttered a postscript attached to the boots; its substance was, "Has Smith the sole to imitate this?" *Smith hadn't.*

"WHO ARE THEY?"

A QUESTION OF VITAL IMPORT.

How often, in our democratic land, the query which forms our caption has caused the aspirants after aristocratic distinction to shudder, and how silent become their voices of high pretension, when, by some unfortunate remark, or the recalling of some reminiscence, they have been forced to take a retrospective glance into the past for a few generations. Happy are they if memory does not wake up a sturdy ancester pounding the leather upon his lapstone, or that necessary craftsman, the tailor, plying his busy needle upon the shop-board. The morbid desire of us republicans to be ignorant of the *vulgar* callings of life, is often very amusing; and the struggles to rake up a pedigree, to give character to growing prosperity, has often caused more trouble and vexation than the building up of a fortune, which it was necessary thus to adorn.

"Who are they?" was the general query at a soiree given by a high United States' officer, at the city of Washington, a short period previous to the death of the lamented General Harrison. The parties who called forth the query were a western member of congress and his highly gifted lady. The member was in the prime of life, of acknowledged talents in his profession, and betrayed, in his manners, the high breeding of a gentleman. A conscious power lent ease to his frankness, and the men of the west clustered around him with pride. His lady, simply attired, attracted all eyes; her *distingue* figure and intellectual face proclaimed her a peerless woman, and when she smiled a ray of heaven's own light beamed forth from human eyes. There was a kindness in her smile which won hearts before they knew her; there was no hollow mockery in it; it came forth from a happy heart, and where its influence fell, good feelings sprung up and sweet thoughts clustered; but—Who is she? Ah, that's the question; and how often the inquiry was passed from lip to lip during that evening! Amid the throng in which they moved, and wherever they lingered, an admiring coterie surrounded them. The husband was a strong man in the political world; had accepted a seat in congress more to gratify his friends than in accordance with his own wishes, and his party felt strengthened by his presence. His lady, ever distinguished at home, was now creating no small sensation at Washington; but—"who are they?" That all-absorbing question remained unanswered, even to the close of the evening, and they departed, leaving it still an "open question."

Judge W. had been seen conversing very familiarly with them, and an anxious company soon surrounded him, uttering the query, "Who are they ?" He informed them, that it was Mr. H. and his wife, Mrs. H., of M——. "Oh! they all knew that, but what was their family ?"

"Upon my life, ladies," answered the good-natured Judge, "I don't know; but if you will only wait until to-morrow evening, I will endeavor to find out."

The task of postponing curiosity, though difficult, was, nevertheless, unavoidable; and the party broke up with a living hope, that ere another day had ended, the important query would be solved.

"Who are you? H.," said the Judge to his friend the next day, as they sat conversing together in H.'s parlor.

"Well, that is a hard question, Judge," replied H.—"but perhaps Mary can answer that question better than I can;" and calling his wife away from a boquet of flowers which she was arranging in a vase; he took her hand in his, as she leaned affectionately over his shoulder, and repeated the inquiry—Who am I, Mary?—the Judge wishes to know."

"I think I can inform you, Judge," replied the wife, "for he is not a whit changed since the day he taught me my first lesson in the 'free school' of L. He is Henry H.—formerly assistant teacher in a down-east *free school*, and now, the Hon. Henry H., of M.; moreover, the husband of Mary H., formerly a *factory girl* in that same town, but now, I need not tell you, Judge, the *Hon.* Mrs. H., also of M.; I have really become quite enamored of this title."

"It is true, Judge," continued Mr. H., "I first beheld Mary at a *free school*, taught her her first lesson, learned another from her eyes, and never became satisfied until I possessed the book, that throughout life I might continue to peruse the beauties of the page. But come, Judge,—now that you have traced our pedigree, give some account of yourself; from what ancient stock have you sprung?—Who are you?"

"I am the son of Adam!" (a laugh here interrupted him,) "not the Adam spoken of in the Bible; I mean old Adam W., a *shoemaker* of Albany, who once used his stirrup rather lavishly upon me, and for which good office, I left him one fine morning, without bidding good by. I will not relate to you the many changes of fortune which befel me, until I found myself upon the *bench*, in a United States' court, instead of the *bench* in my father's shop. Suffice it to say, that my good parent, until his dying day, expressed the opinion that it was a good thing I took to the law early, for I was fit for no *useful purpose.*"

At Secretary E.'s on the next evening, a crowd surrounded the Judge, but all wore upon their countenances an air of incredulity—the Judge's story of the "factory girl" "wouldn't go down."

"It's a fact, ladies," said the Judge; "just about the time I was learning to make shoes these people were in the situations I tell you."

They all pronounced the Judge a wag, and would not believe the story. A matron, more resolved than her friends to sift the truth of the matter, applied to Mrs. H., herself, and told her what a *fib* the Judge had been telling them.

"I assure you it is true," replied Mrs. H.

"Yes, but my dear, the best of families have been reduced," says Mrs. Enquiry, "you are, no doubt, descended from the 'Pilgrim Fathers.' "

"I have every reason to believe so," answered Mrs. H.

"I told you so," said Mrs. Enquiry, exultingly, to her circle of acquaintances; "she is a daughter of one of the 'Pilgrim Fathers.'"

The wheels of government, which had well nigh ceased to move during the pendency of this important question, received a new impetus from the intelligence, and the republic was pronounced "out of danger," for its "heads of wisest censure" had discovered *who they were!*—

THE END.

813R631s
Streaks of squatter life and